Lacey Pinkerton And The Mystery Of The Stolen Mr.E

By Joshua Clark

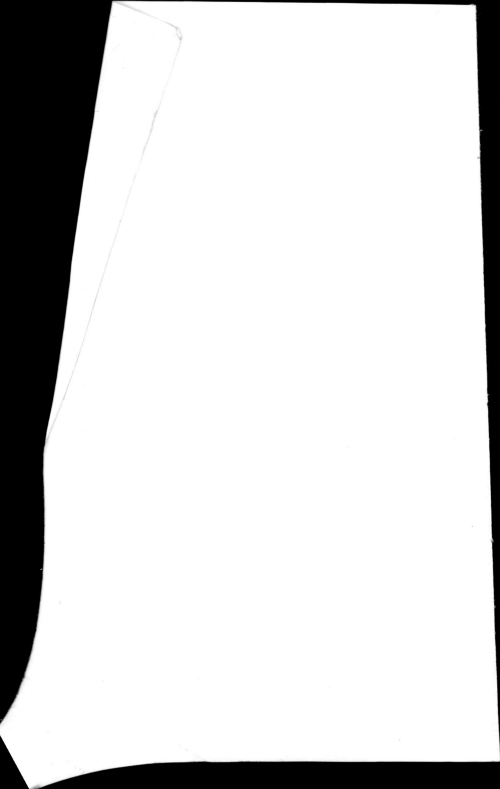

For Madison And Payton

Chapter 1

Summertime Blues

Tick...Tick...Tick... The clock on the wall continued to slowly work its way towards 3pm. There were still thirty minutes of Ticks left. Today was more than just the last day of school. For almost every student in the class, this was the last day of a six year experience. They had become friends, seen each other in and out of casts from various broken bones, supported one another when growing pains hurt

too much and though they may not
realize it now, formed bonds
that would last them the rest of
their lives. They even exchanged
six years of silly Valentine's
Day cards that had things like a
picture of a train that read "I
Choo-Choo-Choose You To Be My
Valentine!" and they *always* came
with horrible little chalk
candies that had absurd messages
like "Be Mine, "I Heart U" and
"Love is Neat". Yuck! But, most
important they had grown
comfortable and felt safe here
at their old elementary school.
Talk on the schoolyard had been
all about the anticipation and
excitement of Summer Vacation
but to Lacey Pinkerton, this was
just about the saddest day of
her life. When summer vacation
was over, she would once again
be the youngest and probably the
smallest kid in the entire
school. Lacey let out a big sigh

and put her head down on her desk, letting her cheek rest on the cool laminated surface.

"Lacey, you're up next. Are you ready?"

It was Mr. Dilford, her favorite teacher of all time. He was having every student stand in front of the class and say a few words about their experiences at the elementary school. He knew from years of sending 5th graders into the world of middle school that they were all a little nervous. He also knew that sharing some of their feelings out loud with their classmates often helped with the stress.

Lacey picked her head up off her desk and walked to the front of the room. She pulled a tiny notebook from her pocket and flipped through a few pages until she found what she was looking for.

"Dear Class," she read out loud,

"I have a few things to say and I don't want to forget anything. As some of you might know, I had a bit of a wild time last week."

Lacey paused and looked up when the class burst out in cheers and laughter.

Sheldon Silverberger shouted,

"*Wild time*?? That's putting it lightly! You saved my house from being robbed and got burglar blood on my porch!"

Then Jimmy Lewis, the school prankster, chimed in.

"Lacey, you solved a huge crime and fought off a dangerous criminal with your dog! You're like a local hero!"

Their teacher interjected,

"James, you know better than to speak out in class without raising your hand! That's ten minutes detention after school!"

Mr. Dilford wrote Jimmy's name on the board under the detention list! Jimmy was stunned and looked embarrassed at being in trouble over such a simple thing. Sheldon didn't raise his hand either! That's unfair, thought Jimmy! Even on the very last day of school, knowing that he'd *never* come back, the teacher was enforcing the rules??

Then Mr. Dilford added seriously,

"Jimmy, you've pranked a lot of people over the last 6 years, me included."

Jimmy looked positively miserable!

Mr. Dilford smiled as he pointed at Jimmy with one hand and erased his name off the chalkboard with the other.

"Now it's finally my turn! Gotcha!"

The classroom erupted in laughs and more cheers. Mr. Dilford had always refrained from any antics like this! And to pull a prank on the king prankster himself? Even Jimmy had to laugh!

Lacey blushed from all the attention.

"Mr. Dilford. please!"

The class settled down and Lacey composed herself.

"Thanks you guys! It was an awesome time working with the police and everything. But, I

couldn't have done it without
Sloan!.... and of course my dog
Newfus!"

Everyone knew about Newfus. Many
of the kids had lost some
valuable items to that giant fur
ball. Frisbees, soccer balls,
kites and even a couple low
flying remote control airplanes!
You name it! If it went over the
Pinkerton fence, it was as good
as gone! Lacey's father had
spent hundreds of dollars
replacing these items so there
were very few hard feelings.

Responding to the many requests,
Lacey told everyone again all
about the case of the missing
ice creams and how she had
really solved a string of home
burglaries. She dramatically
acted out the struggle with the
bad guy, then Newfus's part and
finally she wrapped it up with
Sloan being responsible for

finding all the stolen goods. After the kids cheered again, she brought out a bag of envelops.

"I have invitations for everybody to come to Sloan's surprise birthday party next Saturday!"

Sloan stood up, "What? I didn't know about this!"

Lacey smiled and gave her friend a crisp military-like salute.

"SURPRISE!"

Everyone laughed at this and Mr. Dilford was really happy that the students were in such a great mood.

Lacey continued as she handed out the invitations to everyone.

"It's going to be at Bay Park and there will be food, drinks and lots of games. If you have a

dog, you can bring him or her
for the doggy beauty pageant! I
hope everyone can make it!"

Julie Nicholson asked Lacey,

"Can I bring my cat?"

"No" replied Lacey,

And with a wink at Sloan she
added

"You cannot. Dogs only please."

Lacey loved all animals but knew
that Sloan hated cats. Something
about working one summer at her
dad's pet store Lacey had heard.

Sloan helped her out, now
excited about the *surprise*
party,

"Yes, thank you Lacey. Just
dogs… unless somebody owns a
camel? I love camels! Llamas
would work too. Maybe an alpaca?

Other than that, please let's make it dogs only."

Lacey did like camels so she didn't mind Sloan's added exception. She began to scan the room for anyone that might own one.

A few more people went up and spoke about their time at the school. Some handed out invitations to their own summer parties as well as little parting gifts like candy or in Jimmy Lewis's case gum. Even though it was strictly forbidden inside the classroom, Mr. Dilford allowed everyone to have a piece as long as they promised to discard it properly. He even popped a piece in his own mouth and chewed away! All the rules were out the window today Lacey thought!

After all the students finished speaking, Mr. Dilford stood in front of the class to tell everyone how much he would miss them and that they would all do very well in middle school. The kids were giggling uncontrollably to the point where Mr. Dilford lost his train of thought and had to stop in mid-sentence. He wondered curiously, what could be the source of their sudden amusement? As he took a good look at the smiling faces of his class for the last time he thought to himself "This is the way I will always remember them." All but one of his students were sitting at their desks with bright blue mouths as they enjoyed Jimmy Lewis's *prank* chewing gum. As Mr. Dilford looked over at his reflection in a nearby wall mirror, he laughed at his own blue lips and teeth.

He then turned and with a blue smile bowed ceremoniously in Jimmy's direction.

"Gotcha!" said Jimmy (Without raising his hand first)

Mr. Dilford then turned to the rest of the class and through a big blue smile he told them all,

"Thanks for a wonderful school year! I want all of you to have a great summer! If you _ever_ need me, I'll be right here!"

Brrrrrrrrrrrrrrrrrrrrrrrring…….
.

Summer vacation had begun!

Chapter 2

Duel In The Pool

Lacey answered the phone.

"Pinkerton residence."

It was another RSVP for Sloan's party. So far that made 9 and it was only Saturday. There was still a full week to prepare.

"Ok, Thanks Sandra, I'll see you there with Bronson! He's a handsome fella, he'll be tough to beat! Buh-bye."

Lacey hung up the phone and wrote something down in her trusty notebook.

Bronson was Sandra Baker's chocolate brown Chihuahua. He was an adorable little dog but meaner than any animal Lacey had ever met! One time, back when they were all in third grade, Sandra brought Bronson into class for show and tell. Three kids were bitten and Mrs. Meyers called Animal Control! Since poor little Bronson was too small to actually break the skin, all the kids were unharmed. Animal Control just laughed and Sandra muzzled Bronson with Sloan's pony tail holder. Lacey remembered thinking that he looked like one of those lobsters at the grocery store with its claws rubber banded. She admired his tenacity and, in a way related to the tiny dog. Lacey was glad he was coming.

Mr.Pinkerton often got stuck working Saturdays but today he was in the backyard with flip flops, sunglasses and a hideous Hawaiian shirt. Lacey's mother had thrown this shirt away twice and donated it no less than three times but Lacey's dad was crafty. He somehow always managed to rescue it. One time last summer Lacey caught her mom near their barbecue grill with the shirt, a can of lighter fluid and some matches. Not wanting any witnesses, Mrs. Pinkerton turned, walked back into the house, returned the shirt to her husband's closet and they've never spoken a word about it since.

Lacey didn't care about the shirt, she was more interested in the pop up pool that her dad was filling up for her! The Pinkerton's always wanted a house with a pool but just couldn't afford one yet. So, this was the next best thing. Lacey's dad always put the pool right under the old shade tree so they could climb up on one of its large limbs and jump off into the water. Her mom thought it was too dangerous but that was mostly because of what happened when Mr.Pinkerton tried it out for the first time. They soon discovered that a grown man jumping out of a tree into a shallow pool is terrible idea. When he jumped off the branch, he landed so hard on the slick pool bottom that he slid feet first *busting through* the side of the pool! The water pushed him out like some sort of deranged water slide right into Mrs. Pinkerton's cactus garden! The poor man had thorns and stickers everywhere! After that they repositioned the pool and only kids were allowed to jump.

The pool still needed about an hour to fill up so Lacey made a few more phone calls regarding a last minute present she wanted to get for Sloan. She made her calls, took some more notes and then got into her bathing suit. As she came downstairs there was a knock at the door. At the door was Sloan, beach ball in hand, oversize sunglasses on, and ready for a swim! The two went through the house and out the back door to see if the pool was ready.

Well, the pool was ready alright. So ready that someone else had already jumped in ahead of them! Standing in *their* pool looking happy and relaxed was 250 pounds of black fur, webbed feet and tongue.

"Newfus!"

Lacey wasn't mad, but she wasn't exactly happy either. She yelled out,

"Dad! Newfus is in the pool!"

Sloan added with a sigh,

"Again."

Newfus had his own smaller pool that had hard edges so he could jump in and out without hurting it. Lacey's pool had an inflatable edge. They all knew from experience that although the big dog could easily jump in, there was no way to get him out without destroying the pool. The Pinkerton's seemed to have a bad reputation for destroying pools!

"Dang it Newfus!"

Lacey's dad came out of the garage dragging Newfus's pool behind him.

"Oh Lacey, I'm sorry! I just left for a minute to grab his pool from the shop! I heard a big splash but thought it was you jumping from the tree!"

He went to the pool and placed his hands on the edges. Newfus went to him and with one big lick, managed to wet Mr.Pinkerton's entire face.

"I love you too, big boy but this is what's going to happen. I'm coming *in* and one of us is getting *out*!"

Lacey's dad looked painfully over at the cactus garden and said,

"And I really hope that it's you!"

So here it was, the heavyweight battle of the summer! Already in the ring, weighing in at just over 250 pounds was the defending champion of the pool, Newfus. And *outside* of the pool, weighing in at 230 pounds, dressed in the horrible surfboard and ukulele print shirt was the challenger, Mr.Pinkerton.

A small crowd had gathered and was watching intently. Lacey, Sloan, their mothers, Lacey's brother Lawrence and even Sloan's dad had come over to see the show.

Well, thought Lacey's dad, here goes nothing! And with that he jumped into the water and went for the quick take down. He grabbed Newfus under his front legs and heaved upward. Upward was just what he got! Newfus stood on his back legs and put both his paws on Mr.Pinkerton's shoulders. Even at 6 feet tall, Lacey's dad only stood eye to eye with the huge dog!

"Yikes" Lacey cried out,

"Don't hurt him daddy!"

Mr.Pinkerton looked at her like she was crazy.

"*Me*? Hurt *him*??? Lacey, I can't even move him!"

They wrestled around some more and finally her dad gave up. He rested on the edge of the pool trying to regain his breath. He turned to the crowd and said,

"Why don't I just go buy us another pool?"

Then, just like that, Newfus jumped *over* Mr.Pinkerton and clear out of the pool leaving the inflatable rim unharmed. He reminded Lacey of a killer whale she saw performing at Sea World last summer.

Newfus ran right up to Lacey's mom who had in her hands a great big bowl of his special canned dog food. They had bought several cases of the premium dog chow for when they really needed to get his attention. This definitely qualified.

Lacey's dad called out to her appreciatively,

"Good thinking honey! And just in time too!"

Lacey's mom smiled back and replied,

"Oh, I had the cans opened twenty minutes ago. This is how I got him out of there last year when you were at work. I just wanted to see the show!"

Everyone laughed as Mr. Pinkerton sunk down into the pool resting on the bottom so that just his face stuck out above the surface. Exhausted and a little embarrassed, he remained there for several minutes and contemplated staying there all day.

As the big dog gulped down his special treat, Mrs. Pinkerton gave him a rigorous scratching behind his giant wet ear. Then she leaned down and said affectionately,

"Good boy Newfus!"

Chapter 3

Party Supplies

The next few days were spent between playing in the pool and multiple trips to the party supply store. Sloan had helped Lacey with her birthday just a couple weeks before and she really wanted Sloan's party to be perfect. After all, this was Sloan's 12th birthday. The last one she would have before becoming a teenager! Yikes, thought Lacey!

On Sunday the girls had gone to some neighborhood garage sales and Sloan's mother took them to a giant thrift store outlet. They didn't have much luck at the garage sales but at the giant outlet store they found wigs, dresses, fancy old shirts and a dozen hats. They bought several belts of various colors and designs that if you trimmed them up would make fancy show collars.

This doggy beauty pageant wasn't going to be some simple contest that was based purely on breeding and good looks. This show would have several categories for the pampered pooches to compete in. Along with Best In Show, there would be prizes for Best Dressed, Best Hair, Cutest Dog, Biggest Dog, Smallest Dog, Sweetest Dog and Worst Breath. Lacey was pretty sure Newfus would win *one* of these.

Today was Wednesday and Sloan's mother had just finished washing all the items from the outlet store. Lacey's brother Lawrence was helping trim down the belts and add holes so they could fit like collars.

"Newfus is a lousy model." Lawrence complained.

"He's too big! Some of these belts actually need to be longer to fit on him! We need a real dog to see if this stuff is the right size."

Lacey scoffed at her brother's obvious lack of respect for her shaggy friend,

"He *is* a real dog! Don't listen to him Newfus, you are just the right size."

As he left the house Lawrence shouted over his shoulder,

"Yeah, for a *grizzly bear*!"

Sloan helped Lacey place a wig and hat combination on Newfus's head. They both were pleased with the look.

"Ha!" Said Sloan

"I've never seen a grizzly bear look this good with blonde curls and a summer hat! Newfus, you look glamorous. You just might win two categories at this thing!"

As Sloan removed the wide brimmed summer hat she covered her mouth and gagged a little.

"Make that three categories! Oh Newfus, yuck! Your breath stinks!"

Lacey, ever the stickler for facts and evidence, leaned over and gave the big dog a dramatic sniff.

"Yep, that's disgusting. Worst Breath is *not* a prize I want him to win!"

Sloan gathered up the hats and other accessories.

"L.P., let's go to my dad's store and get him some Denti-sticks and a new toothbrush. While we're there we can measure some of the dogs for show collars. Plus, I want to pick out some good prizes! For Biggest Dog, my dad already ordered a giant bone from the butcher shop."

The girls both looked at Newfus and laughed. He was lying down and taking up a good third of Sloan's living room floor. He looked up when he heard the word "bone" but quickly assessed that there wasn't one to be found.

With a loud sigh of disappointment and a thud he rested his head back on the floor.

Sloan's mom agreed to drive them to the pet store. Her car was perfect for 4 people but not 3 people and a Newfus. The big fella had to stay behind but was allowed to stay in the cool air conditioned living room at the Stevens' house. They loaded up in the car. Sloan selected some good music and they were off to the pet store.

Chapter 4

The Microchip Voice Thingy

When they arrived at the pet store Sloan's dad was talking to a man that was installing some sort of device above the front doorway. The man finished tightening something and called out to Sloan's dad,

"That's the last adjustment Mr. Stevens. Just turn it on and it should work. The volume control and power button are by the cash register like you wanted."

Mr. Stevens thanked the worker
and then turned to his family
looking pleased at the
unexpected visit.

"Well, to what do I owe this
great surprise?"

"Hi Daddy, we need some Denti-
sticks for Newfus, his breath
smells like garbage."

Lacey looked a little hurt at
the insult but then agreed,

"Yeah, it's pretty gross. Will
the Denti-sticks help? Or do we
need something stronger?"

Lacey looked over at a selection
of large brushes designed for
scrubbing everything from
carpets to horse hooves.

"Can we use one of these on his
teeth? With a lot of
toothpaste?"

Sloan's dad laughed,

"Well, his mouth is about the biggest I've ever seen on a dog but his teeth need a special brush. I have some good ones on this aisle over here."

Just then an electronic sounding female voice sounded over their heads,

"Hello ROXY, welcome to Second Chance Pets!"

A lady holding a small fox terrier had walked in the door and was looking quite confused. Sloan's dad hurried to assist her,

"Hello ma'am, that's our new....."

Mr. Stevens paused as he tried to remember the exact name of the darn thing, but he couldn't remember so he said,

"...It's our new M.V.T. system"

This of course stood for
Microchip Voice Thingy.

"It picks up any pet's microchip
that comes through the door and
then announces the pet name
that's registered on the chip."

The lady looked impressed.
"M.V.T. System" sounded very
technical she thought.

"Wow, that's a nice touch! Very
High Tech! Now, do you have any
gourmet chicken liver flavor
rawhide treats? They are Roxy's
favorite!"

Mr. Stevens led the woman down
an aisle that had hundreds of
packaged dog bones and treats.
There was also a bin full of
slightly used dog toys and chew
toys.

Second Chance Pets was not your
typical pet store. This was
something that had never been

done anywhere before. 10 years ago Mr. Stevens worked for an agency that rescued animals and then tried to find them homes. The agency lost funding due to budget cuts and Mr. Stevens had to leave his job. He found an inexpensive location down on Culver Street and rescued as many animals as he could from the agency's kennels. Second Chance Pets started selling, at an affordable price, rescued dogs and cats as well as pet supplies and toys. Sloan's mom was buying used pet toys from the big thrift store outlet and some of the toys were brand new with the tags still on them. Eventually, they built up enough business to carry new pet accessories, foods and toys but the animals were always "Second Chance". The store moved to the new location when the old building became part of the site for the new mall.

After Mr. Stevens had helped the lady and rang her up at the register they heard the female robot voice again,

"Good-bye ROXY! Thank you for shopping at Second Chance Pets!"

Lacey asked Mr. Stevens if it would just continue to greet somebody if they walked in and out of the store?

He said he didn't know.

Then she asked what happens when someone walks out at the *same time* someone walks *in*?

Again, he said he didn't know.

Then she asked what would happen if someone walked in with *two* pets at the *same time*?

And once again Mr. Stevens politely answered that he didn't know.

Sloan's dad knew Lacey very well and had developed a high tolerance for her many questions. He always tried to answer them to her satisfaction. Then, after he had to explain to her that he could <u>not</u> put a microchip in her just so she could try out the new gadget, Mr. Stevens told the girls that he had some good news for the party.

"I just brought in a litter of German Shepard puppies that were abandoned down on the docks. The mother must have been on a ship and hiding the pups in the cargo hold. The ship left and took the mother but not these 4 puppies. They are actually eating solid food and old enough to adopt. You can take them to your party and let people who don't have dogs 'borrow' them for the contests. Then, if anyone wants, they can adopt them."

Lacey and Sloan screamed with delight,

"Oh Yes! Thank you daddy!

"Yes, thank you Mr. Stevens!"

The girls visited with the young German Shepherds and played with them for a bit. Then they grabbed Newfus's dental hygiene supplies and headed out the door.

"Goodbye LACEY PEENKERTOON, Thanks for shopping at Second Chance Pets!"

It was the female robot voice! Did she have a microchip! It must have been the school nurse! She always suspected the school was spying on her!

Sloan's mom and dad were laughing uncontrollably. Then her dad walked up to Lacey and reached in her shopping bag. He pulled out a tiny capsule.

"It's a microchip that I put in your bag Lacey…Just a little joke, you can keep it."

They all laughed and then loaded up into the car. On the way home Lacey wondered to herself what would happen if she swallowed the microchip and then ran in and out of Mr.Stevens' store. She smiled at the thought of that robot voice going berserk trying to keep up with her running in and out. That would be a good prank for sure! But then she decided that she really liked Sloan's dad and probably drove him crazy enough without any practical jokes. Besides, it would surely make her sick

anyway. She put it in her pocket
for safe keeping.

Chapter 5

The Greatest Birthday Party In The History Of The World, Ever.

It was a beautiful day at the Bayside Park. Both girls' dads had gone to the park early to secure a good spot with picnic tables and a view of the water. Lacey's dad set up a grill while Sloan's dad put together a large corral to keep all the dogs in. A couple of other parents showed up to inflate balloons and set up the decorations.

Lacey's dad looked around. The place was really starting to look great. He filled the barbecue with charcoal and checked the coolers for enough drinks and ice. He then went to his truck to start unloading the folding chairs and tables he had rented. Wow, he thought, I wish my parents had given me a party like this when I was a kid!

Sloan's dad helped him unload the truck. Mr.Pinkerton asked him,

"I've been meaning to ask you something. Sloan really loves dogs and well, it seems like she would have one as a pet. You help so many people adopt dogs, is there a reason you guys don't have one yourselves?"

Mr. Stevens smiled and answered,

"Yeah, you'd think with all the choices she has at the store she would have picked one by now. The truth is she just hasn't connected with any of them. I'm guessing that when she sees the right dog, she'll know. No offense but I really hope it's smaller than Newfus."

Mr.Pinkerton looked over at where Newfus was napping in the grass. A bird had landed on him thinking the dog was a furry boulder. Newfus didn't move, or care.

"No offense taken, when we rescued him we thought he was just a big _four_ month old Springer Spaniel puppy. We even named him 'Springer' for a little while. We had no idea he was a _two_ month old Newfoundland! Lacey's the one who figured out what he really was, and made us change his name."

Mr. Stevens laughed,

"Yeah I remember that day. Lacey and Newfus hit it off right away. That's what Sloan is waiting for. I hope someday she finds it, even if it *is* a 250 pound bear dog!"

When Lacey and Sloan arrived at the park, they couldn't believe how awesome everything looked. Lacey's mom started covering the tables with party table cloths while Sloan's mom started mixing up a huge batch of fruit punch. On one table, per the girls' request, there was nothing but a bright red sheet. This was the "awards table" where all the prizes for the different contest would be kept. There were bones, rawhide chews, liver snacks, squeaky toys and other little goodies that Mr. Stevens and Second Chance Pets had donated to the party. The girls laid the awards out in order of size and then set the table up along the edge of bushes that lined the outside of the park. That way the dogs would have a harder time sneaking up and "awarding" themselves.

Lacey found a good strong tree to put Newfus's chain around. The chain was way heavier than she really needed but some people were still a little nervous about the big dog. They just felt better when they saw he was tied to a tree with a boat's anchor chain. Oh well, she thought, at least he has a big shady area to sleep in.

Sloan walked over to Lacey and the two of them surveyed the entire scene. They agreed that it was all perfect. The pen that Sloan's dad had made for the dogs was huge! And he even made a smaller corral off to the side as a "time out" zone if any dogs misbehaved. He had food and water set out and even set up a couple "pup tents" where they could rest in the shade. Mr. Stevens was probably the biggest dog lover Lacey had ever known. She hoped that the human guests would have as good a time as the pampered doggies! Sloan assured her that it was going to be a great time for everybody.

The girls went over the plans that Lacey had written in her notepad. Lacey read them out and Sloan confirmed.

"20 water balloons for the balloon toss?"

Sloan quickly counted the colorful water bombs that were kept safe in a large plastic tub.

"Check!"

"20 burlap sacks for the sack race?"

Again, Sloan counted the supply.

"Check!"

"Doggy dress up supplies and accessories?"

Sloan poked through a plastic tub containing the wigs, belts, hats and other items.

"Check!"

Lacey smiled,

"Special prize for Biggest Dog?"

Sloan made a face as she picked up a large bone that was actually a femur from a cow wrapped in plastic by her father's butcher.

"One giant dinosaur bone with gross bloody meaty stuff on it. Yuck! …I mean, Check!"

Lacey continued down the list of categories.

"Contest award for Best in Show?"

"One luxurious doggy brush and a box of liver treats. Check!"

"Contest award for Best Dressed?"

"Penguin squeaky toy and beef flavored rawhide. Check!"

"Award for Best Hair?"

"Chicken flavored rawhide chews. Check!"

Lacey finally got down to the last two categories.

"Contest award for Worst Breath?"

Sloan wondered to herself just *who* would be the judge for this category? I'll volunteer my dad she thought. He'll like that.

"One bag of Denti-Sticks and a doggy toothbrush. Check!

And finally,

"Contest award for Smallest Dog?"

Sloan walked to the end of the prize table flipping up the corner of the red table cloth. She then looked under the table. All she saw was an old bag of peanuts someone had dropped. She looked up at a passing seagull and violently shook her fist at it.

"Check MINUS! It's gone! It was right here next to the other small prizes! Dang bird must have taken it!"

Lacey looked up and watched as the prime suspect landed on the water just fifty yards away. She turned to Sloan,

"What was it, a bone? Birds would steal a dog bone I think."

Sloan eyed the bird suspiciously then answered,

"No, it was a little squeaky toy shaped like a smiling carrot."

Lacey gave her friend a puzzled look,

"Sloan, why would a seagull take a squeaky toy that looks like a smiling carrot? Or *any* squeaky toy??"

Sloan tilted her head as she watched the bird fly away,

"Maybe he thought it was a real carrot?"

Lacey shrugged,

"Oh well, we'll just have to cut a category or find a new prize. But, everything else is here! All we need now are the guests.

How long before the party starts?"

"One hour" Sloan replied.

And the two girls sat on a bench while they waited for the fun to start. Newfus walked over to them and laid down at their feet for another nap. The two friends leaned back and put their feet up on the big dog. Lacey put her hands behind her head and stretched in the warm sun,

"This is going to be the greatest birthday party in the history of the world, *ever*!"

Chapter 6

The Guests Arrive

The first car to roll up and drop off a guest was Aluna Kariuki. She was a tall beautiful girl and arrived wearing a colorful African dress. Aluna was born in Kenya but had come to the United States when she was five. Aluna, while a very pretty name, in Kenyan means "come here". Her parents soon discovered it was very hard to train their dog without confusing their daughter at the same time, and vice versa. Her parents and everyone else just called her Ally.

Ally's dog was a Rhodesian Ridgeback and black lab mix named Hooper. Hooper looked just like a jet black Rhodesian Ridgeback. He went over to Newfus cautiously and they gave each other a sniff. Lacey looked concerned that they might not get along. Ally told her it would be alright,

"Rhodesian Ridgebacks are bred in Africa to hunt lions, not bears."

The girls laughed and this seemed to ease the tension with the dogs too as they soon began to play and wrestle.

Jennie Carlson was the next guest to show up.

"Come on Buford! This will be fun. You're embarrassing me!"

She was pulling on a leash that was attached to a very stubborn English Bulldog. Her mother parked their car and came over with a small bag of something. When she handed the bag to Jennie, Buford's ears perked up and he immediately started trotting along.

Sloan called out,

"Hi Jennie! I love your dog! I guess he changed his mind and wants to come to the party after all."

"Hi Sloan! Hi Lacey! No, he's as stubborn as a mule but he loves this!

Jennie held up the small plastic bag.

"Bacon!"

Now Jennie had the attention of *all* the dogs at the party. She looked terrified as Newfus trotted over and sniffed the bag. He stood just a little taller than she did! As if he could sense she was scared, he gave her a nice big lick on the cheek.

Jennie's mom screamed as she was certain Newfus was about to eat her daughter,

"Jennie!! For God's sake, <u>Give him the</u> <u>bacon</u>!!!"

Lacey intervened,

"It's ok Mrs. Carlson, he won't hurt her. Newfus No! That's not your food!"

And with his head down, Newfus trotted away sadly wondering why they had *showed* him the bacon, if they weren't going to *give* him any delicious bacon?

After Lacey chained Newfus to his tree and gave him a couple of his own liver treats, Jennie relaxed a little,

"It's ok Lacey, he can have some of it as long as he doesn't eat *me*!"

Lacey laughed,

"No, but thanks though. He's gonna get enough treats later. Also, if you don't want all the dogs sniffing in your pocket, you might want to put the bacon on that table with the contest prizes."

Jennie figured that was a good idea. After breaking off a piece for Buford to help get him into the corral, she put the bag of bacon on the table with the bones and other doggie prizes. When she set the bag down, she thought she heard a rustling in the bushes just beyond the

table. She looked but didn't see
anything. Jennie figured it was
just a squirrel or some little
birds. She decided to place a
medium sized rock on the bag
just in case one of the little
creatures decided to try and
steal it.

More guests started arriving and
the corral proved to be ample
size to house all the dogs
comfortably.

Jimmy Lewis walked up to them
with his female Australian
Shepard/Lab mix that could catch
frisbees! Her name was Sheela.
It was really amazing to watch
as Sheela jumped high into the
air and sometimes did backflips
to catch the flying discs! Sloan
noticed that Jimmy was dressed
nice and didn't have any pranks
or sarcastic comments. He was a
lot different outside of school.
He even let Sloan and Lacey take

turns throwing the frisbee for Sheela who caught it every time!

Sheldon Silverberger didn't have a dog but borrowed one of the abandoned German Shepherd pups. He immediately fell in love with the young dog and within minutes Mrs. Silverberger was filling out the papers and writing a check to Sloan's dad. Per Sloan's request, half the proceeds from the sale of the abandoned pups was going to the local no-kill animal shelter. She wanted to support the shelter so they could care for the older dogs and cats that Second Chance Pets couldn't take in.

Everyone stopped when they heard a shrill voice scream,

"OW, my finger!! That stupid dog bit me!!"

It was Peter Carlson, Jenny's bratty little brother.

There next to him was Sandra Baker, holding a snarling little brown bundle of muscle, Bronson. Sandra was yelling at Peter.

"I told you he doesn't like to be poked! Go poke your own dog!"

Then she turned to Sloan looking embarrassed,

"I'm sorry Sloan! He's really a good dog but he's always smaller than the rest and gets scared….and sometimes *bitey*."

Bitey, Lacey thought? Now that's a good word! And she wrote it down in her notepad so she'd remember. She liked Bronson and now that he'd bitten Jenny's bratty brother, she liked him even more!

Sloan liked him too.

"I know what he wants. Just a little love, that's all."

Sloan reached gently over and gave the dog a soft scratch. His head was so small that she could scratch him behind both ears with one hand. Then all of a sudden, he laid his ears back playfully and jumped right into her arms! Bronson wagged his little tail and licked her face. Sloan was giggling and turned to the sniveling little boy,

"Yeah, he's vicious! We better chain him to the tree with Newfus before he kills us all!"

Peter's mother made sure that the tiny dog hadn't done any real damage. Of course he hadn't. Little Peter was sent off to play with his bulldog who looked bored.

I hope he doesn't poke Buford, thought Lacey.

Jenny could tell what Lacey was thinking and told her,

"Oh don't worry, Petey knows better than to poke *him*. Buford bites *a lot* harder than a Chihuahua!"

Jenny called out to her brother. When he turned to look she held up her hand with one of the fingers bent down to symbolize a missing finger.

He yelled back,

"I know, I know!"

Lacey laughed and asked,

"Does he get…. 'bitey'?

Jenny smiled back and shook her head

"No, just with my brother."

The girls laughed as they walked over to look at the growing collection of dogs in the corral. Sloan didn't want to put Bronson in with all those bigger dogs and asked if she could hold him for a while longer. Sandra had never seen the little dog take to anyone like that before and was happy to let her.

"Hold him as long as you want, he likes you!"

Three more kids showed up with another 2 siblings. The remaining German Shepherd puppies were loaned out and those without a dog just helped the others with the dressing and preparations. *Now* it was a party!

Lacey's dad set up a stereo with big speakers and a P.A. system so he could address the crowd and officiate the games. He also would be using the microphone to announce the winners of the doggie beauty pageant. But right now, it was time to play some music! The girls always used Sloan's mom's mp3 player because she seemed to like the same kind of music that they did. Plus, she would let Sloan and Lacey download music onto it so they had some really good playlists.

The boys and girls all took part in dressing the dogs up in various costumes. The parents took lots of pictures to capture the moment and later post online.

Nobody got photographed more than Buford in his sunglasses and one of those Rastafarian hats with the fake dreadlocks sticking out! He was perfect because he just sat there posing. He liked the attention so he sat up tall loving that everyone was so interested in him.

Sloan carried Bronson through most of the games. They did ok in the potato sack race but got the poor little guy soaked in the water balloon toss! (She really should have thought that one through) She decided to give the Chihuahua a break and asked Sandra if she could let him relax in the "time out" area. Sandra said that would be fine. When she set him down he cried and whined for her to pick him back up.

Lacey walked over and looked down at the little dog. It was tough going to new places where everyone was bigger than you. Lacey thought about her upcoming matriculation to middle school. She felt bad for the tiny guy so she decided to get him a little treat. She found Jenny adjusting her bulldog's sunglasses and fixing his long dreadlocks so they draped over his muscular shoulders.

"Jenny, Buford looks amazing! Do you think he'd mind if I gave Bronson a little bit of his bacon?"

Jenny waved at her,

"Of course, take all you want. I only brought it so I could get him to be social. He's doing fine now. Just leave one little piece so I can get him to come when it's time to go."

Lacey thanked her and together with Sloan, headed over past all the festivities to the prize table. When they looked where the bacon had been it was gone! And two more prizes were missing! No dogs had even come close to the table.

"Sloan! Go get everyone over here right away. I have an announcement to make"

Sloan turned down the music and got the microphone from her dad. She called for everyone to put all the dogs away and meet her over at the prize table. Everyone gathered around. Lacey reached into her pocket and pulled out her "Forensic Investigation Team" badge. She held it up for everyone to see,

"This table is now a crime scene! And this party just became..."

Lacey raised the microphone to her lips and said in her deepest detective voice,

"...a *Mystery*!"

Chapter 7

The Cutest Little Mystery

Lacey's mom rolled her eyes,

"Cheese and crackers Lacey! Not at Sloan's party! Please? It was probably just some birds or a squirrel."

Ally stepped forward,

"No Mrs. Pinkerton, look at the peanuts on the ground. If it were a bird or squirrel, it would have eaten those nuts for sure!"

Lacey smiled at Ally,

"She's right. This is a burglary! I'll stake my badge on it!"

Once again her mother rolled her eyes and groaned. Then Lacey noticed the group was looking over at *her* dog.

"And will everyone please stop looking at Newfus! He's been chained up the whole time. Sheesh!"

Poor Newfus she thought. Every time something comes up missing, everyone thinks he ate it! Ok, most the time it was true, but not today!

When he heard his name the big dog popped his head up. He wanted to know what all the fuss was and started crying for Lacey. She turned and looked at him.

"Great, now you've hurt his feelings."

Lacey thought for a second and then,

"Does everyone agree that Newfus wins the prize for biggest dog?"

Jimmy Lewis gave a quick answer,

"Uh, duh Lacey. He's three times as big as any dog here. He obviously wins."

Everyone agreed, it wasn't exactly a "spoiler alert".

Sloan could tell where this was going and picked up the big bone.

"I've got this, Lacey."

Sloan unwrapped the bone, ran over to Newfus and made him sit before placing the prize in his giant mouth.

"There you are you big baby, and just so you know...you're going to win Worst Breath too! Yuck!"

Back at the table, the parents had lost interest and went back to socializing, cooking and eating. The kids however were all following Lacey's every word and wanted to help solve this mystery.

Ally had an idea,

"Hooper is a natural tracker. If you have something that he can get the scent from, he'll track it down."

Jenny picked up the rock from the table.

"I put this rock on the bag of bacon, it might have some of the bacon smell on it."

They brought Hooper over and Ally had him smell the rock. The black dog immediately put his nose to the ground and started following the scent. The kids all followed behind. He sniffed along the edge of the bushes until they broke open and exposed a little path. Ally had Hooper on a leash but he was pulling to go into the bushes. She wasn't sure what to do and all the grownups were on the other side of the park.

"Should I let him off the leash so he can follow the scent?"

Everyone agreed that she should so she unhooked Hooper's collar. He jumped into the bushes and before any of the kids could climb in after him there was violent sound of barking, snarling and other scary noises. Then there was a yelp! Hooper came flying back through the hole in the bushes and stood panting next to Ally.

The kids were a little scared now. Something had really scared Hooper and he was a pretty big dog! Whatever was in there had taken a small chunk out of poor Hooper's ear! Lacey felt angry that Ally's dog was hurt. Then she realized that there was an even bigger dog at the party.

Lacey turned to Sloan,

"Go get my Newfus!"

"Now hold on just a minute Lacey."

It was Mr.Pinkerton who had come over when he heard the noise.

"You don't know what's back there. It could be fox with rabies or maybe an injured animal."

At the thought of an injured animal, Sloan ran and got her dad who was already heading towards all the commotion. He took a look at Hooper who looked a little shaken up. The kids told him what had happened.

"Alright, let's see what we have here. I need to take a look at Hooper and see if he's been bitten by anything."

Mr. Stevens examined Ally's dog while she nervously watched. She thought to herself, Why had she let him off the leash? She knew better!

"Well, it looks like he's been bitten on his ear. I'll have to go try to find what it was so we can check it for rabies."

Ally started to cry. Lacey and Sloan both put their arms around her. Lacey assured her that Sloan's dad was the best and would make everything ok.

After getting some gloves and a blanket from his car, Mr.

Stevens told the kids to wait
while he went into bushes.
Lacey's dad followed behind and
although none of the other kids
noticed, he had also gone to *his*
truck to get something. He
caught Lacey looking at the lump
from the gun in his pocket so he
leaned over and told her,

"Just in case."

The two men were in the bushes a
few minutes when Sloan's dad
popped his head out. He was out
of breath and had leaves and
spider webs all stuck in his
hair.

"Sloan sweetie, please go get
some liver treats and a bottle
of water."

She followed his instructions
and quickly returned with the
items. Her dad took them from
her and said,

"Now follow me…..Just Sloan for now. Everyone else stay back."

Lacey was very upset,

"No way! Where's my dad? I'm coming too! We're partners and partners don't split up!"

"Alright Lacey, you can come too. Your dad *said* you wouldn't stay behind. Just be quiet and don't make any sudden moves. Now follow me."

And the three of them went past the bushes and into the forest of trees behind the park. As they approached Lacey's dad he motioned for the girls to move slowly and be quiet. He was sitting on the ground next to a small palm tree. The blanket was placed curiously over part of the base of the tree.

Lacey whispered,

"What's under the blanket?"

Then Sloan asked,

"I'll bet it's a wolverine! Is it? Is it a wolverine?"

Mr.Pinkerton chuckled,

"No Sloan it's not a wolverine. I promise you I wouldn't be sitting here if it was!"

Then Sloan's dad called her over to the tree. He gently lifted back the blanket. There in a small hole he had dug at the base of the tree was the saddest little dog Sloan had ever seen. He had backed himself into the hole so that just his head was sticking out. The little dog had a long snout covered in dirt and what looked like a little blood mixed in. His ears looked two sizes too big for his little head and he was shaking uncontrollably.

Sloan's dad explained,

"He's scared Sloan. He doesn't have rabies, but he is sick. He's dehydrated."

Sloan looked like she was about to cry. Before her father could stop her she just leaned down and picked the dog up cradling it in her arms like a baby! She turned to Lacey,

"L.P., open the water and hand it to me."

Lacey did what her friend asked and handed the bottle to Sloan.

"Easy now little guy, I'm not going to hurt you…..just take a little sip…."

The little dog's tongue went crazy trying to get the water from the bottle.

Lacey's dad pulled out his pocket knife,

"Here, hand me the bottle. Let me try this,"

He cut off the top part of the bottle so the dog could easily get to the water and handed it back to Sloan.

She held the water and the little dog drank it all.

Mr. Stevens gently stroked the little dog's head. The rage and fear had left his eyes and he seemed to relax a little.

"It's a Doxie. Looks like a purebred too. If I had to guess, I'd say he can't be older than 8 months or so. He's really just a puppy, I wonder what he's doing out here all by himself? I'll take him back to the store and get him cleaned up. We can check him for a microchip too."

Lacey looked in the hole by the tree. All the stolen items were there, including the smiling carrot. She leaned down and gathered it all up and they walked back to the party.

Ally was very happy to learn that Hooper would be fine and Lacey handed out all the remaining prizes.

Jimmy's acrobatic, frisbee catching dog Sheela won Best in Show. Not only was she a beautiful dog, she was the only dog there that could do an amazing trick.

Buford won best dressed and growled when Peter tried to remove his sunglasses.

Hooper won Best hair for his distinctive black ridge of hair that ran down his back.

Newfus won Biggest Dog *and* Worst Breath.

The Cutest Dog award went to
Sheldon's new German Shepherd
puppy.

Last but not least was the prize
for Sweetest Dog. Sloan insisted
this prize go to Bronson. This
made Sandra very happy.

While the awards were being
passed out, Sloan had cleaned up
the little Dachshund and got him
to eat some real dog food. She
held the little dog up and
looked into his big eyes,

"I don't know where you came
from or what your name is, but
we're gonna fix you up."

Her dad walked up and fed the
little guy a liver treat. He
looked at Sloan and Lacey,

"Well girls, looks like you have
a real little mystery on your
hands."

Lacey's eyes lit up,

"That's what we'll call him, 'Mr.E'! He's our little Mr.E. If we don't find out his real name, we can call him something else. But for now, he should be Mr.E."

Sloan liked it. She held the dog for the entire rest of the party, only allowing Lacey to hold him for a few minutes while she opened presents. The little dog wouldn't let anyone else hold him so the girls just handed Mr.E back and forth when they needed to.

The cake was eaten, the parents were loading everything up and Sloan had thanked everyone for the best party she ever had. The girls sat down on a park bench, exhausted from the long day. Newfus lumbered over and laid down, doing his job as footrest. Sloan held a sleeping Mr.E and Lacey leaned back with her feet up on Newfus's head. The party was finally over.

All of a sudden, a man driving a truck and huge horse trailer came to a screeching halt right up and onto the grass in front of them! The man went around to the back and opened the doors of the trailer. When he came around from behind the trailer Sloan gasped.

The man called out to Lacey,

"Sorry I'm late, I got a flat tire on the freeway. Did I miss the party??"

The man was walking with a giant saddled beast but it *wasn't* a horse!

Lacey turned to her best friend,

"Oh yeah, I rented you a camel! Happy Birthday!"

Chapter 8

Good Morning, Pickles!

Sunday morning, everyone slept in. At the Pinkerton house, Newfus slept out on the patio with his giant cow femur. Lacey was snug in her bed loosely clutching her mini baseball bat, though she never dreamed about chasing criminals any more. Lacey's brother, Lawrence was staying at a friend's house for a few days to watch some sort of Kung-Fu movie marathon. Over at the Stevens' house Sloan was

sleeping soundly and in her arms
was little Mr.E. He was clean,
fed, given lots of water and
finally a little bed to sleep
in. The little bed remained
unused because from the time she
got home, Sloan never put the
dog down.

Mr. Stevens was downstairs
drinking his coffee and
searching for articles online
for anyone missing a miniature
dachshund. He hoped he wouldn't
find any. He knew it would break
Sloan's heart if she had to give
up the little dog so soon. She
had agreed the night before to
put posters up around town and
that they would look for Mr.E's
owner for two weeks. If they
didn't find anyone missing the
little doxie by then, she could
keep him.

After a little while, both
households woke up and were

getting ready for the day.
Lacey's mom went out to print up
a bunch of fliers at her office
while Lacey went with her dad to
the hardware store to get some
staples for their staple gun.
They loaded up in his truck and
headed to the store. As they
passed Culver Street Lacey saw
that there were banners and
signs all over announcing that
the area was the future site of
the new mall. Finally, she
thought, they are tearing down
those abandoned buildings!
Lacey's dad was the Assistant
District Attorney and part of
his job was to go after the
developers that originally
bought up all these buildings.
He had been trying for over a
year to make them build the mall
they promised. Up until now the
abandoned buildings had done
nothing except attract crime.

Her dad saw that she was smiling,

"We finally won in court and the judge said they had to begin demolition immediately. There's going to be a scale model of what the new mall will look like in the center of the old mall. I saw a police bulletin that said there was going to be some sort of big art display there for publicity. The mall asked for some off duty policemen to come and help protect one of the pieces that's worth over $200,000.00!"

Lacey had never seen any artwork that was worth that much! Most of *her* best stuff was on the refrigerator being protected by her mom's magnet collection.

"I'll bet it's something really great! I can't wait to see it!"

Her dad chuckled,

"Well, I saw a picture of it and I hate to tell you Lacey, but it's hideous. It's solid gold and looks like some kind of deranged baby's face puking up jewels."

Lacey made a face,

"That's disgusting. Sloan and I need to see it right away!"

Her dad knew he'd never hear the end of it if he didn't tell her she could go see the hideous display so he agreed to take her that evening as soon as she had put up all the fliers.

In the hardware store they walked past a row of stools and a counter top that looked more like a restaurant than a place that sold tools. Lacey's dad explained that years ago the hardware store had been a place where people would often meet and have a soda or an ice cream.

Now the only soda came out of a self-serve cooler behind the counter and sadly, there was no more ice cream. They walked to the aisle where the staples were stocked and found what they needed. When they got back to the front of the store, an older man behind the counter greeted Lacey's dad with a big smile,

"Good Morning Pickles! How is my favorite Pinkerton Detective today?"

Lacey's dad blushed and he cleared his throat.

"Ahhhemmm…..It's 'ADA' Pinkerton now Mr. Mueller. But you know you can just call me Morris. And this is my daughter Lacey."

Mr. Mueller came around from behind the counter to shake Lacey's hand,

"Well, ever since your dad here saved my life back in his detective days, I've been calling him Pickles. I'm sure you've heard the story a million times. He's a real hero you know!"

Mr.Pinkerton started to put up his hand to protest, but the older man just waved him off.

"Oh alright Pickles… I can see I'm embarrassing you so I'll shut my big old trap and introduce myself. Lacey, my name is Gus Mueller and this unorganized mess is my store. It's very nice to meet you. I hear you are quite the detective and a hero yourself!"

Now it was Lacey's turn to be embarrassed,

"Well sir, it's very nice to meet you too. I've only really solved one case so I have a lot of catching up to do! Plus it was my dog Newfus that was the real hero. But I've never heard *any* stories about my dad saving someone's life."

Then with a giggle she asked,

"And why do you call him Pickles?"

Her dad groaned and then sat on one of the vinyl covered swivel stools that lined the counter.

"Mr. Mueller, please….we're in a hurry. You can tell her about it some other time."

But it was too late. Lacey was already sitting down at her own stool, ready to hear the story. Her dad had no choice but to grab a couple of root beers from the cooler and let her enjoy a cold drink while Mr. Mueller told his tale.

"You see Lacey, about 11 years ago or so, when your mom was pregnant with you, your dad was a detective assigned to investigate a string of armed robberies in this area. A few local business owners had been roughed up and robbed. Every day before going home, your dad would stop in at every store and check up on us. Well, one evening just before closing time your dad had gone on a food run to help your mom with some cravings she was having. He stopped in here carrying a shopping bag with Rocky Road ice cream, orange juice and a jar of pickles. He was standing just a few feet from where we are now, next to the register. I remember he had set his bag on the counter so we could talk for a bit. All of a sudden a man ran into the store with a pair of pantyhose pulled over his face waving a gun around! The guy starts yelling at us and tells us not to move or he'll shoot us dead! Then he points the gun at me and tells me to give him all the cash out of the register. Well, I didn't spend twenty years in the United States Marine Corps to be threatened by some punk with underwear on his head! I told him go suck a rotten egg and get the heck out of my store!"

Lacey was listening intently,

"Then what happened?? Did he leave??

Well, not exactly. Part of being an old man is that I sometimes forget that *I'm an old man…* and not as tough as I used to be. Well this robber was a wanted man in four states and he didn't mind there being one less old hardware store owner in the world. He raised his gun up to my face and was going blow my head off! Before he could pull the trigger, your dad smashed him over the head with a jar of pickles! *Pickles*! Darndest thing I ever saw! The funny thing was, your dad, a detective at the time was carrying his service revolver! He had a gun the whole time but chose to use the pickles! Ain't that right Pickles?"

It was all too true thought Lacey's dad. If only he had hit the guy with the ice cream, maybe Mr. Mueller would be calling him "Rocky" instead. That would be much better he thought.

Mr. Mueller slapped Lacey's dad on the back and let out a hearty laugh. Mr.Pinkerton's face was bright red and he had long finished his root beer. He thanked Mr. Mueller for the staples, the root beer and the story. As they were leaving the store he turned to Lacey,

"Your mother does <u>not</u> know about this and she doesn't need to, does she?"

Lacey didn't like keeping secrets from her mom, but she figured that he was just trying to prevent his wife from worrying. Besides, it was so long ago.

"No problem, your secret is safe with me….Pickles."

Her dad just shook his head,

"Please get in the truck Lacey."

Chapter 9

Scared to DEATH!

When Lacey and her dad got home, Lacey kept her word and never mentioned the pickle story. Her mom handed the stack of flyers to her and a large satchel that fit on Newfus's back. They often used the saddlebags for carrying loads when they went on picnics. She tied the two sided pack onto the dog and then secured it with a belt under his belly. Lacey loaded up the fliers and staple gun in one side and some bottled water in the other. She gave Newfus a little liver treat and then walked him over to Sloan's house. Newfus always felt important when he was wearing his packs and pushed right in through the front door to show everyone. The big dog flung open the Stevens' front door nearly knocking over poor Mr. Stevens!

"Whoaaaaa big fella! Slow down…Yes, I see you have your back pack on! Good boy! Gooood boy!"

He gave Newfus a good scratching on his head and called for Sloan to come downstairs. When she did she was holding Mr.E under one arm. The little dog looked very comfortable until he saw Newfus walking up to Sloan to say hello. Apparently the little doxie had no concept of size. He jumped out of Sloan's arms and

charged at Newfus. The little
dog was snarling and barking as
if he wanted to tear Newfus
apart! Newfus looked at the
little dog and tilted his head
to the side as if he was trying
to figure out what the doxie was
saying. He looked at Mr.E, and
then he looked at Lacey.
Finally, he put his big paw on
the little dog's head as if he
could *squash* him quiet. But Mr.E
wouldn't be silenced so easy. He
bit Newfus's paw and then hung
on! The big dog didn't know what
to do! It didn't really hurt but
it *was* very annoying. Newfus
looked like he got his paw stuck
in a wiener-dog shaped
mousetrap! Everybody watched in
silence with mouths open as they
were unsure of what to do.
Finally Newfus limped over on
three legs to Lacey, held up his
paw and barked as if to say

"Will you please remove this? I have no idea what it is."

Sloan walked up and started to pet Newfus to show Mr.E that he was a friendly dog. To everyone's surprise, it actually worked and the doxie responded immediately. Mr.E dropped to the ground, then jumped up onto Newfus's back. From there it was an easy leap right into Sloan's waiting arms. Her dad was quite impressed.

"It wasn't that he wanted to fight with Newfus, he was protecting you Sloan! That's a smart little dog. And pretty tough too! I've seen Newfus swallow things bigger than him! He's got quite a personality!"

Sloan rubbed the little doxie's head and said sadly,

"Well we better go put up these posters in case his owner is out there looking for him. Hey, L.P., did you bring enough bottled water?"

Sloan reached over and opened the pouch containing the water but as soon as she got the flap open, Mr.E jumped *into* the bag! He stayed low and wormed his way into the very bottom of the pouch as if to hide.

Lacey walked over to see what the little guy looked like way down in that pouch. She hoped he could breathe ok. He looked up at her wide eyed and alert as if waiting for something. Well, she thought, he looks comfortable. Lacey gently closed the flap but didn't buckle it.

"I guess he likes it in there. Seems weird for him to just jump right in. It's almost as if he was trained to do that. Very interesting."

The plan was to walk all the way to the mall and post the flyers on every corner along the way. It was only about a mile walk to Second Chance Pets so they planned a pit stop there for lunch with Sloan's dad. Lacey had told Sloan all about the Golden Barf Baby. They decided that after lunch they would walk the additional mile or so to the mall and see it. Lacey's dad said he would meet them along the way and later give them a ride home.

The first poster went up on a telephone pole right across the street from their houses. Lacey struggled with the staple gun. She finally gave up and Sloan had to help her.

"Dang it Sloan, I hate being so little sometimes! I hope you don't have to do stuff like this for me at middle school."

"Don't worry L.P., you've got all the muscle you need right there in that head of yours! I'm the one that should be worried, I only got a C+ in math!"

Lacey felt a little better and watched Sloan put in the last staple.

"Ok, I guess you're right. You help me with the heavy lifting and I'll help you with the heavy trigonometry."

Sloan looked at Lacey as if she had just spoken Chinese,

"The *what*??"

Lacey laughed and now felt much better about her staple gun failure.

"It's Math, don't worry I'll show you later. So, how many posters is that so far?"

Sloan gave her a funny look and replied,

"One."

"That's correct! Good job! See, you'll be a math star in no time!"

Sloan gave Lacey a playful shove into Newfus.

"Oh hardy *har har* Miss Pinkerton! Very funny!"

Sloan and Lacey laughed as they made their way to the pet store, putting up flyers along the way.

The flyers had a picture of Mr.E, a description of him and where he was found. They also had the phone number to Second Chance Pets. Along the top of the flyer, in big bold letters were the words "FOUND DOG".

After about an hour they arrived at the pet store. Sloan's dad had agreed to drive on ahead and meet them there with lunch and to fit Mr.E with a collar. They had put up most of the flyers when they arrived at the store. Sloan handed Lacey a bottle of water from Mr.E's side of the pack and gave the little guy a pat on the head. He poked his head up looked around and then ducked back into the pouch.

Newfus loved Second Chance Pets. It was the only store that allowed him to come see what the humans were doing instead of tying him to a tree or in the truck. It made him feel very important! The girls knew the drill. Before Newfus could go in, they had to go in first and make sure there weren't any customers that would freak out when they saw him. The coast was clear and they walked him inside.

"Hello NEWFUS welcome to Second Chance Pets!"

It was the microchip voice thingy and it scared the heck out of Newfus! First Newfus barked his loudest bark, then Sloan screamed because Newfus's big mouth was right behind her head and finally, out from his hiding place jumped Mr.E barking and growling at everything that wasn't Sloan! He circled the girls three times before jumping up onto Newfus's back for a better look. Once he was satisfied it was all clear he jumped into Sloan's waiting arms.

Sloan's dad was still holding his chest from the scare Newfus had given him,

"Darn it Newfus! You almost gave me a heart attack! And look at poor Oscar!"

They all looked at a large bird cage in the center of the store. Oscar was an African Grey Parrot that had been neglected and now resided at the pet store permanently. He was too neurotic for anyone to ever have as a house pet. Oscar's defense mechanism was to hang by his feet, spread his wings out and play dead. For some reason, this is how Oscar thought a bird would look if it were to die from fright. So there he was, gently rocking back and forth like a feathery fruit bat pretending that he had died. Mr. Stevens threw a blanket over the cage and assured the girls that Oscar would "come back to life" in a few minutes.

Chapter 10

Is *This* Paranoia?

"That dog really loves you Sloan! I don't want to get your hopes up but I checked every lost dog website and agency for anyone within fifty miles. Not one person has reported a lost mini dachshund. I can't believe that someone would lose this little guy for as long as he's been out there and not report it. I guess we'll find out soon enough. Who's hungry? I have pizza and dog food set up in the back….your choice!"

As they all walked to the back of the store you could faintly hear a squawky voice from under the covered cage...

"Baaad dog...baaaaaaad dog! Squaaaaaaaaaaaaaaaaaaawk!"

Mr. Stevens laughed,

"It's a miracle! Oscar's alive!"

He removed the blanket and followed everyone to the back for some pizza.

Sloan's dad never noticed the black van that had pulled up in front of the store. It stayed parked in front for quite a while with the engine running. Nobody got out and you couldn't see anyone through the dark tinted windows. When Lacey's dad pulled up and parked behind it, the van quickly sped away.

Mr.Pinkerton walked in and followed the smell of pizza to where everyone was eating.

"Do any of you know who was driving that black van out front?"

Nobody else had even seen it. Then Sloan's dad started walking to the front of the store,

"I must have forgotten to turn on the Open sign. I'm normally closed on Sundays so they might have just been some confused customers."

Then Lacey walked up to her dad,

"Daddy, did you get his license number?"

"You bet I did, Lacey. Here, copy it down in your notebook, just in case."

Lacey loved it when her dad treated her like a real

detective, even if it was just a suspicious van. She copied the numbers down and then read them back to him.

Sloan's dad smiled at them both.

"You two are just paranoid, I'm sure it nothing."

Lacey whipped around pulling out her honorary investigator badge and sticking it right up to Mr. Steven's nose!

"Oh yeah, is *this* paranoid?"

 Then she held out her tiny notepad.

"How about this, is *this* paranoid! They don't just give these out to everybody!"

Her dad jumped in,

"Easy now Lacey, don't get all worked up. Mr. Stevens didn't mean any harm. Besides, he's probably right. We are being a little paranoid. Let's finish eating and head to the mall."

He turned to Sloan's dad to apologize, making sure that the girls couldn't hear,

"Sorry about that. I don't know how such a little girl can get so worked up! She's going to make one heck of a detective someday. I'd hate to be a perp sitting across from her at an interrogation, that's for sure!"

Mr. Stevens walked over to Newfus and opened the pouch to check on Mr.E. He picked up the little dog and held him up for Mr.Pinkerton to see.

"It's quite alright. I love Lacey's big personality. It reminds me that it isn't easy to be the smallest and sometimes you need to bark a little to be taken seriously."

He set the little dog on
Newfus's back and opened the
pouch. Mr.E jumped right back
in.

Lacey's dad thought that was a
pretty neat trick.

"How did you teach him to do
that?"

Mr. Stevens explained that the
dog had quite a few little
personality traits that led him
to believe he had been trained
for months and there were
probably a few more tricks they
had yet to see.

After locking up the front door
and making sure the Open sign
was off, Sloan's dad followed
everyone out through the back
door, set the alarm and locked
it. It was only about a half
mile or so to the mall so they
all decided to walk together.

They had walked for about 10 minutes when Lacey stopped.

"Daddy, come tie my shoe."

"Lacey, you're a bit old for me to tie your shoe. Besides, you're wearing *sandals*."

Lacey tried to talk seriously through a fake smile and clenched teeth,

"Daddy, come tie my shoe, Please."

Her dad sensed something was wrong and as he walked up to her she stuck out her foot for him to "tie" her sandal. When he knelt down and took hold of her foot she whispered,

"Daddy, look over my shoulder over by the dumpsters at that restaurant."

While still awkwardly pretending to tie Lacey's sandal,

Mr.Pinkerton looked at where Lacey had told him. There just beyond a pair of blue dumpsters he could make out the front end of a black van.

"Daddy, is that the van you saw?"

"I can't be certain, but I know one way to find out, stay here."

And just like that, her dad jumped up and started walking toward the van!

Mr. Stevens called out,

"Morris? What the heck are you doing??"

As the van's tires squealed and it pulled away disappearing around a corner, Lacey's dad answered him,

"Well, I hate to say it but if Lacey's instincts were right, a

van full of 'paranoid' just
followed us for half a mile!"

Chapter 11

The Golden Barf Baby

Lacey's dad called the plate numbers into the police dispatcher and they said they would call him with any results. As strange as it seemed, the entire group was now determined to go see what was now being called "The Golden Barf Baby". When they got the mall there were two armed guards at the door. Lacey's dad said they were off duty police officers and had worked with one of them a long time ago. He walked over and spoke with the guard for a while and then came back to the group.

"I gave him the description of that van so he can let the mall chief of security know about it. He said that two nights ago the night security guard ran off a black van fitting that description."

Lacey was very interested in these details.

"Did you say *the* guard? As in singular? There's all these guys during the day and only *one* guard at night?"

As usual, Lacey's dad was impressed with his daughter's attention for detail.

"That's right Lacey. Great observation, I asked the same exact question! When the mall closes and all the security

doors are shut from the inside,
it becomes completely
impenetrable from the outside.
The only way in after the mall
closes is this main door. And
there's a guard here all night
long."

Lacey smiled triumphantly at
being commended on her "great
observation" and then they all
filed into the mall. One really
nice thing about this mall was
how pet friendly it was. There
was even a large fenced area
where you could let your dog off
the leash. It cost five dollars
an hour but an attendant made
sure your dog was happy while
you shopped the stores where
dogs couldn't enter.

They walked past the food court.
Mr.E's tiny nose poked out just
a bit as he sniffed the scent of
fresh corn dogs. Then he
hunkered back down into his

little pouch. Finally they reached the display in the center of the mall. There were paintings and sculptures that were all encased in protective plexiglass. Then they saw it. Resting on a stone pedestal surrounded by glass was the most hideous sculpture that any of them had ever seen. Lacey's dad was right. It was a baby's solid gold head with the mouth opened way wider than a real mouth could ever open. The eyes were some sort of blue jewels and they were rolled back and looking straight up as if the thing was being strangled. Then there was the barf. A jewel encrusted river of gold was splashing out of the mouth and hung suspended as if this golden barfing baby had been frozen in time.

A grizzled old man with a long shaggy beard was also admiring the display and walked over to Lacey.

"It's from India. It represents the God of Unexpected Fortune. Don't you think it's beautiful?"

Lacey was more than happy to reply,

"Well sir, that painting of the lady over there, I think *that's* beautiful. This dog right here.."

And she patted Newfus on the head.

"…I think *he's* beautiful. In a way, even your crazy white beard is kinda beautiful. But the thing they've got trapped in that glass box is about the most disgusting thing I've ever seen."

And with that she took Newfus by his leash and walked away.

The man looked at Lacey's dad
but Mr.Pinkerton just shrugged
and said,

"Sorry pal, I'm with her on this
one. That thing *is* ugly. Is it
really worth $200,000?"

The man was staring at the
golden head as if it was the
most gorgeous thing in the
entire world.

"$253,500 to be exact, and worth
every penny to someone who *knows*
fine art. Of course most of that
is in the value of the gold and
jewels themselves. But the art
is one of a kind, There's
nothing like it in the entire
world!"

Mr.Pinkerton had heard enough
and decided to go join the rest
of the group. He turned to tell
the old geezer thanks but he was
long gone. The rest of the group
was walking up to the scale

model of the new mall. They were all admiring how cool the new mall was going to be when all of a sudden Mr.E jumped out of his satchel and ran across the mall floor! He ducked behind a potted palm tree that looked kind of like the tree they had found him hiding near at the park. When Sloan and Lacey caught up with him he was curled up and wagging his little tail. In the spot where he was laying there was a chewed up baby's pacifier, some used corn dog sticks and what looked like a piece of torn carpet that he was using as a bed. Mr.E had been here before!

"I don't get it L.P., this is his little nest but when did he build it, and why was he here?"

"I don't know Sloan. He must've been hiding out here before he went to the park. Maybe the added security scared him away.

Look at how he's sitting up and
wagging his tail! It's as if he
was trained to go right to this
spot and now wants your
approval. Tell him he's a good
dog."

Sloan did and Mr.E's tail wagged
even more as he curled up into
his little nook. She reached
down and picked him up.

"Ok, you don't live in the mall
and eat garbage any more, got
it? You live with us now."

And with that she put him back
in Newfus's saddlebag and
scratched his little head.

"Good boy, now just relax. We're
almost done here."

As Lacey, Sloan, Newfus and Mr.E
all walked through the mall they
noticed a hallway that had an
Exit sign. Sloan looked back to
where her dad was talking with

Mr. Stevens and was about to ask him why the mall didn't need a guard outside this door at night. He was too far away so she decided to walk down the hallway a bit and check it out. There was a large sign on the wall that read "Deliveries and Authorized Personnel ONLY". She turned to Sloan,

"Surely they don't mean us, right? I mean, we're just looking to see if there's a hole in their security plan."

"I don't know L.P., let's just take a quick look and then ask your dad."

So the girls walked down the hallway and past the warning sign. When they reached the door, they saw it was massive! Lacey tried to push it open but it was too heavy.

"Come help me open this door Sloan, I've almost got it."

"Fine but if we set off some alarm I'm running away and blaming Newfus!"

Sloan put her shoulder against the door and braced to push. Lacey decided they would count down and then push together,

"Ok, ready?"

Sloan nodded yes.

"Here we go…..ONE……...TWO…………..THREE!"

The girls both pushed hard on the big door and it flew open much easier than they had anticipated! The girls went tumbling out almost falling face first onto the ground outside. Before they could turn around, the big door swung shut behind them!

Lacey ran to the door and pounded it with her tiny fists.

"Cheese and Crackers!! We're locked out! How do we open this door Sloan?"

The big door had no handles or knobs or any way to open it from the outside. It even had steel flaps on the edges so that when it was closed you couldn't see the gap in the door's frame.

They turned around to look and see where they were. It was the other side of the mall where employees sometimes parked. It was pretty empty and only one car was driving through. Lacey grabbed Sloan's arm.

"Sloan, we need to get back inside now!"

It was the black van and it was driving across the parking lot right towards them! Sloan started banging on the door yelling for her dad, Then Lacey joined her screaming for someone to come open the door! The van was just a hundred feet away and picking up speed!

There was a loud clicking noise and something that sounded like air whooshing through a tube. The door slowly opened and they rushed inside.

They were still screaming as they passed Mr.E who was jumping up and down on Newfus's back and wagging his little tail. Putting both their shoulders into it, they slammed the door shut and ran to get their dads.

As they ran, Sloan asked Lacey who had opened the door.

"I don't know! There's nobody over here!"

It was quite a mystery indeed.

Chapter 12

Dog Gone Heartbreak

The girls got to Lacey's dad first. Sloan's dad was at the mall office trying to arrange a pet adoption booth for next weekend. Mr.Pinkerton was talking to one of the off duty policemen that was about to start his guard shift when the girls both ran up to him screaming at the same time,

"The black van! The black van!"

The policeman radioed to the other guards to meet them all at the back delivery door. When they got there the guard did something unexpected. Instead of pushing the door, he pushed a big green button on the wall. The door swung open. Under the button, leaned up against the wall was a chair. The girls decided that it must have been because of the chair that they didn't see the button.

Sloan held the door open while Lacey's dad and the guard searched for any sign of the van. Because the driver of the van hadn't really committed any crime yet, there was not much they could do except make a report about the suspicious activity. Newfus was nudging at Sloan with his big wet nose and then at Lacey while letting out a low whimper. Lacey put her hand on the big dog's head.

"What's wrong Newfus? Are you hungry again?"

Newfus started whining louder and again nudged Sloan. Sloan could tell something was wrong.

"Maybe the pack is bothering him. He's been wearing it for a few hours now. Can we take it off of him for a bit?"

Lacey agreed and Sloan reached to get Mr.E out of the pack. When she opened the flap, the saddlebag was empty!!

"He's not in here L.P.! He's gone! We have to find him!"

The little doxie was nowhere to be found. They searched the entire mall and behind every potted plant. They found several plants that had been used as little doggie hideouts but they were all empty.

Sloan started to cry. And then Lacey started to cry. Finally Newfus started to cry and let out a low sad howl. He could sense when his girls were unhappy and he didn't like it.

Sloan's dad walked up and immediately put his arms around his little girl and asked what happened. They told him the whole story about the door, the van and then about Mr.E running away.

Sloan's dad called Mr.Pinkerton over to talk to him.

"Morris, I take back what I said earlier about you two being paranoid. I think that van belonged to a couple of dog nappers! They weren't following us, they were following the dog. Who knows, they might have been after Newfus too!"

When Lacey heard that she threw her arms around Newfus's big neck and squeezed.

"They better not even think about it! And we're gonna get back Mr.E too! Daddy, is it a crime to steal a dog even if the dog isn't really yours?"

Her dad had to think a moment. It was actually a very good question.

"Well, technically no but didn't you put a collar on him with the store's info?"

Sloan's dad said that he had and that he also inscribed "Mr.E" on the tag so they'd have something to call him.

"Well if that's the case then that dog belongs to Second Chance Pets and can now be reported stolen. I'll call it in."

Lacey had dried her tears and was getting ready for business. She got out her badge and her notepad.

"Sloan, we're gonna solve this crime! The mystery of the stolen Mr.E will not be a mystery for long!"

Sloan added with a tearful half smile,

"You'll 'stake your badge on it'?"

"Better than that Sloan, I promise! Now let's get to work. I know the first thing we're gonna do!"

After they looked all around the outside of the mall one more time, they loaded up and drove home. Lacey's mom had a label maker that printed up sheets of labels at a time. Lacey asked her to make up three sheets of

labels with nothing but the word
"**STOLEN**" in big bold letters.
Next her mom drove them to every
place where they had posted a
flyer. On each flyer where the
words "FOUND DOG" were they put
a label over the word "FOUND" so
they now all read "**STOLEN** DOG".

Lacey's mom said she'd make more
flyers with the updated message
when she went to work in the
morning. They drove by the mall
one last time before it got dark
and then home. Lacey promised
Sloan that if her dad found out
anything she would call
immediately. She explained that
there was an APB (all-points
bulletin) out on the van and
that Sloan's dad had emailed a
description of Mr.E to every
animal agency in the state. None
of this seemed to make Sloan
feel any better.

Lacey's mom felt so bad for her daughter's best friend but didn't know what she could do. On the way home she pulled into the parking lot of a small convenience store and parked the car.

"Just wait in the car girls, I'll be right back."

Mrs. Pinkerton came out of the store with a paper bag and when she got in the car she turned to Sloan.

"When Lacey solved that big burglary case last month, all the papers reported the story. The company that makes these got so much publicity that they decided to start selling them in stores."

Sloan opened the bag and inside were two Double Fudgy Fudge Ice Cream Sandwiches!

"I know it won't make things better but maybe this will cheer you up a little."

The girls both thanked her and unwrapped their ice creams.

Sloan smiled as she bit into the treat. It did cheer her up, a little.

Chapter 13

How To Wash A Newfus

Sloan barely slept that night. In the morning Lacey had something for them to do that might make her feel better. One thing that Sloan really enjoyed was helping Lacey give Newfus a bath. This used to be a near impossible task because Newfus would just lie down as soon as you got out the hose. To solve this problem, Lacey and her dad constructed a shower station where you could walk Newfus onto

a pad, hook his collar to a
chain that was secured above and
then use a couple of long
handled scrub brushes to get him
clean. The chain didn't hurt him
but it did make the big guy
stand up for the whole process.

Sloan walked Newfus into his
shower contraption while Lacey
went into her dad's shop to get
the brushes and soap. She
grabbed two brushes and then
reached into a case of shampoo
bottles. They had to buy the
shampoo from Sloan's dad by the
case because it took exactly one
whole bottle to wash an entire
Newfus! When Lacey got back to
the station, Newfus was hooked
to his chain and wagging his
tail. He liked the scrub down
and *loved* water! Lacey laid out
five small plastic cups and
poured the shampoo, distributing

it evenly in all five. Each cup was labeled for various body parts on Newfus. This was a very organized procedure! By this time Sloan had completely soaked all of his fur with the garden hose. They used a special hose attachment that had plastic "fingers" so they could get to Newfus's thick undercoat. Together they applied each cup of soap followed by a vigorous scrubbing. Soapy froth flew everywhere as Newfus wagged his giant tail.

After a good rinsing off of both the dog and themselves, the girls went back to Sloan's house. They asked Sloan's mom if she would drive them to Mrs. Pinkerton's office to pick up the new "Stolen Dog" flyers. She of course said she would and called ahead to make sure the flyers were ready.

They left Newfus to dry in the morning sun. Several birds flocked over to the dog wash station and were pecking at the clumps of black fur that were scattered on the wet ground. The local birds had discovered that Newfus shed a lot during these washes and used the bits of dog hair to help insulate their nests. Just about every bird's nest in a 2 block radius had a little bit of Newfus in it!

It was a short drive to Mrs. Pinkerton's office and before long they had the new flyers in their hands. They posted them everywhere they could think of and put a few at Bayside Park where they had first found Mr.E. As Sloan stapled the last flyer to a telephone pole across from the mall she let out a long sigh.

"Oh Lacey, I hope somebody finds him and calls. I'm so worried about him. At least with all these flyers they won't be stealing any more dogs around here!"

Lacey started thinking and something just didn't add up.

"Sloan, when we first found Mr.E your dad checked every website and organization within fifty miles to see if there were any reports of a missing doxie. Then he said that very few dogs and *no* dachshunds at all were reported missing."

Sloan nodded and said,

"Yep, he even emailed all his friends that own pet stores around the state. Someone did steal a tank full of snakes, but no doxies."

Lacey continued with her theory,

"If there's organized dog stealing going on, you'd think there would be news about it somewhere. We put all those posters up and I didn't see any other missing dog posters. I need to call my dad and ask him something. Let's head home."

Sloan was a smart girl but she knew Lacey's wheels were turning too fast for her to catch up. She decided to wait and let her friend explain it all when the time was right.

When they got home Sloan went to her own house with her mom to make some sandwiches and a veggie snack plate. Lacey went next door and called her dad. She had to wait a few minutes while his assistant found him. Lacey hoped he wouldn't be too busy for what she needed. When he finally picked up the phone she asked him to find out if that black van had been reported in connection with any other crimes. She was relieved when he told her that he thought she might be onto something. He said it might take some time but he would bring the information home with him tonight.

She left out through her front door and checked on Newfus who was now dry but still lying in the sun. She gave him a good belly rub to make sure he was completely dry then walked with him over to Sloan's house.

Mrs. Stevens had lunch all spread out on the table for them. There were ham and turkey sandwiches cut into neat little squares. Also, on an oval serving dish she had a pile of cut up carrots, celery, broccoli and snap peas. The girls were very hungry so they dug right in while Lacey explained her newest theory.

"Ok, let's go over the facts. First, we know that Mr.E had been in the mall before and had at least one special hiding place. Second, nobody has reported him missing before us. Third, there is a suspicious van that was already chased out of the parking lot once by security, *before* we ever found Mr.E. And last, there is a door that can only be opened from the inside yet it opened twice without anyone around to press the button. It opened once to let us *in* and then again to let Mr.E *out*!"

Sloan was confused but was starting to follow where Lacey was going……kind of.

"What does it all mean L.P.?"

"I'm not sure but my gut tells me that Mr.E is somehow connected with the black van. Like maybe they already stole him once and he got away. Or something like that, I'm still working it out."

Lacey tapped the side of her head with a celery stick.

"Come on brain…figure this out!"

Sloan looked around the table and then waved her carrot stick like a wand,

"I know what's missing!"

Lacey threw her hands up in the air with anticipation,

"What Sloan? What's missing??"

Sloan shook her carrot stick at Lacey and replied,

"Ranch Dressing."

Chapter 14

It's *Not* The Corn Bread

When Lacey's dad got home he found that Lacey had converted the dining room into some sort of evidence processing headquarters. She had a large dry erase board with little notes stuck all over. There were lines drawn in various colors connecting the notes. On the table there were several newspapers laid out. One of which was missing most of the front page because Newfus had tried to read it first.

"What's all this? Did you find some new clues?"

"Hi daddy. I've been putting up possible theories on my investigation board but they all stink! Did you find out anything about that van?"

Her dad explained that in the last few months there had only been one report of a black van involved in a robbery. The robbery took place at some business that made jewelry.

Lacey insisted on hearing all about it in case there was some detail that would be important.

"Well, according to the detective who works burglaries in that area, the thieves didn't get away with any actual jewelry. The items they took were for melting metals and setting stones. They would only be valuable to someone that was in the jewelry business. The whole thing was dismissed as a botched jewel heist."

Lacey was writing all of this down on a sticky note and then added it to her investigation board.

"Lacey, I hate to say it but these guys are probably long gone. With so many people looking for that little dog, they won't stick around here."

He looked over towards the kitchen.

"Is your mom home yet, I'm starving."

Lacey said that her mom hadn't got home yet. Her dad decided that *he* would make them some dinner and asked if Lacey would help. Of course she agreed. She loved to help in the kitchen! She always felt that cooking was just a series of experiments that you got to perform and then test on yourself.

Lacey's dad decided they would have baked chicken and corn bread. For some reason he loved making the little cornbread loaves and considered his version to be something of a specialty. He liked to pour in half the batter and let it cook for just long enough for it to thicken. Then he would take it out of the oven to add honey. After he laid in a few stripes of the honey he poured the rest of the batter over the top. When they were completely done he'd take them out of their little molds and serve them up.

Lacey mixed up the batter while her dad prepared the chicken. He dusted the bird with his special blend of herbs and spices then covered it with foil and put it in the oven. Next he took the corn bread mold out of the cupboard and applied some non-stick cooking spray. Lacey poured the batter into the molds filling them all just half way.

After they put the corn bread in the oven to cook for a bit, Lacey's dad went upstairs to change out of his work clothes. When he came back down he was in his shorts, a t-shirt and flip flops. Lacey liked seeing her dad dressed like this. It made him seem like a big kid and he was more relaxed. He grabbed a pot holder and took the partly cooked loaves out of the oven, setting them on the stove. He grabbed the bottle of honey and carefully applied three stripes to the inside of each loaf.

"Ok Lacey now pour the rest of the batter in gently, just half way. You don't want to spill any of that golden goodness!"

Lacey looked down at the little golden loaves as she poured the batter gently sealing in the honey. Then she stopped and set the bowl down.

"Daddy, may I go use your computer please? I need to look something up on the internet."

"Of course sweetie. You aren't looking up new cornbread recipes are you?"

She laughed and said,

"No, I'm curious about something completely different but kind of the same. It's about the case. I'll just be a few minutes."

"Ok, but if you're looking up cornbread recipes….."

Lacey playfully snapped back at him,

"It's not about cornbread!"

Her dad put up his hands in surrender,

"Ok, ok…..Go ahead then."

When Lacey returned to the kitchen her mother was home and helping prepare some vegetables. Somehow when her dad cooked dinner, he always forgot to make vegetables. He often insisted that tater tots were a food group and counted as a vegetable, but he couldn't find any in the freezer.

Lacey had to take all of her investigation supplies down and set the table for dinner. She then put glasses out for everyone and poured iced tea all around. Before she sat down she ran outside and gave Newfus a big bowl of food. She knew he smelled dinner cooking and didn't want him to feel left out. When the people food was ready they all sat down and ate. Mrs. Pinkerton talked about a house she just sold and was very happy. Lacey's dad said he had a decent day but really only wanted to talk about the corn bread. Finally when they were done eating and all the dishes were put up, Lacey asked her dad to look at her investigation board that was now set up in the living room.

"Daddy, I've added everything up and I think I have an idea what the black van people are up to. Do you think the chief of security at the mall would add some more guards this week if I convinced him he needed them?"

Her dad was looking at the sticky notes and trying to follow what is daughter was getting at.

"Well Lacey, if it's about the art display, I wouldn't worry too much about that. The mall will be closed in about ten minutes and my buddy on the force told me that they are moving the whole exhibit by armored car at noon tomorrow, even the Golden Barf Baby."

"Cheese and Crackers daddy! We have to get to the mall now! They're going to try and steal the Golden Barf Baby tonight! And I know how!"

Chapter 15

Stakeout

"Lacey, I don't know about all that. You and Scooby Newfus over there did a great job catching the Ice Cream Truck Bandit, but I think we should leave this one to the police. Besides, there's no way into the mall except the front door. If they break in anywhere it will trigger the alarms."

"Daddy, you have to trust me! If I'm right, they've already got a man on the inside!"

"Ok, ok, I trust you. Give me just a minute to change, then we'll go."

Lacey's dad went back upstairs to change into something more appropriate. Some dads take their daughter's fishing or shopping. He wondered how many dads took their children to stake out a major crime? Oh well, he would never let her get close enough to be in any real danger. When he got back downstairs there were now two children and a giant dog waiting for him.

"Sloan, sweetie, you'll have to ask your parents before I can take you. It could be dangerous. And Newfus? Well, I guess that's fine."

He didn't want to admit it but he felt a little safer when the big dog was around.

"Don't worry Mr.Pinkerton, I already asked my parents and they said as long as I stayed in the truck I could go. Lacey told me what's going on."

"Well I'm glad she told you because I'm still not sure myself."

They all got in the truck. Newfus and Sloan sat in the back and Lacey sat in front giving instructions. She told her dad to park off to the side so nobody would see them. Her dad pulled the truck up behind some trees and turned off his lights. From where they were parked, they could see the back door where the girls had encountered the black van. There was a flood light directly over the door so they could easily detect if anyone went near it. They were far enough away to be hidden by the trees and the darkness. It was the perfect place to stake out the scene.

Sloan rolled one of the back windows down a little so Newfus could get some air. The big dog wasn't sure why they weren't getting out of the car so he just laid down across the back seats with his head on Sloan's lap.

They sat and watched for any sign of the black van but the parking lot was quiet. Suddenly, Newfus popped his head up and started to let out a low growl. It scared Sloan and she wrapped her arms around his neck and buried her face in his fur. Someone was out there, but where? Lacey's dad rolled the window up in case Newfus barked and gave away their position. He reached back and patted Newfus on the head.

"Easy boy, its ok buddy."

Then he saw poor Sloan hanging on to the dog for dear life. Her face was totally hidden by the thick black fur.

"Sloan, its ok, don't be scared. There's nobody out there."

But was that true, he thought? The girls weren't convinced either. They all pressed against the windows of the truck scanning the parking lot for any signs of the black van.

Then the light above the mall door went dark! Someone had knocked out the light! There *was* someone out there and they were on foot!

Lacey whispered to everyone,

"This is it! Now wait for it….that door is going to open any second….from the *inside*!"

Sure enough the darkness surrounding the door was now penetrated by a sliver of light. When the door opened, they all watched as two shadows crept through the doorway and into the mall! The door closed behind them and the area went black.

Lacey's dad was already on the phone with the police. Lacey and Sloan listened as the dispatcher told him that it would take several minutes for units to get there. He thanked them and hung up. The girls were looking at him anxiously wondering what to do. The safe thing to do was to just sit and wait for the police to arrive, but then he looked at Lacey and saw the determination and courage in her eyes. There wasn't enough time to drive around the front to get the security guard. He decided they could at least go block the door with his truck until the police arrived.

Besides, he had to do *something*, Lacey had already pulled out her badge!

Chapter 16

The Inside Man

Mr.Pinkerton drove the truck towards the door and was going to put his bumper against it when Lacey stopped him.

"Daddy stop here so the door can open. We need to do something first!"

"Why? If I pull all the way up I can block them in and they'll have no way out."

"Because daddy, they have a
hostage! Don't be mad, I'll be
right back!"

And before he could get his seat
belt off and stop her, Lacey had
jumped out of the truck and was
running for the mall door! As he
got out of the truck to retrieve
her, he heard the *back* door open
and watched as Sloan jumped out
to join her friend! Great, he
thought! The only one that
stayed in the truck was the dog!
This was pretty much the
opposite of what he wanted to
happen.

"Girls!, get back in the truck!
NOW!"

Sloan was now pressed against
the door and tapping on it! What
on earth are they doing he
thought? He ran over and
snatched up both girls and
carried them back to the truck.

Then he heard the door open behind him. He turned to face whoever was coming out, feeling slightly vulnerable as he stood there with a small girl under each arm. He called out for the only thing he could think of,

"NEW-FUS!"

The big dog, sensing something was wrong, jumped out of the truck and ran up to him growling at the opening door. He set the girls down behind Newfus and pulled his revolver from his pocket. Mr.Pinkerton stood in front of everyone pointing his gun at the door, ready for whoever came out!

"Daddy wait, don't shoot! Look!"

At the bottom of the door, poking his little head out was Mr.E! When Sloan saw the little dog she ran and picked him up, tears streaming down her face.

"Good boy! Very good boy!!"

Lacey's dad told the girls to get in the truck. They grabbed Newfus and Mr.E then loaded into the back. Mr.Pinkerton jumped behind the wheel and pulled the truck all the way against the door, sealing the burglars inside.

The back seat was a bit crowded so Lacey climbed up front with her dad. He looked at her and smiled.

"Inside man, huh? Well, when you're right, you're right."

Lacey's dad leaned over and gave his little girl a kiss on the forehead.

"Lacey, don't ever scare me like that again! That goes for you too Sloan! This is real and you could get hurt."

"I'm sorry daddy I guess I just acted without thinking. My gut said it was the right thing to do. Kinda like smashing a jar of pickles on an armed robber's head."

Her dad laughed,

"Well, it's not quite the same for a 10 year old girl, but I know what you're saying."

Just then the police arrived with sirens blaring. They had come in full force. The whole parking lot was lit up with blue and red lights! Lacey's dad received a call on his cell phone from his policeman friend asking him to just stay where he was for a few minutes longer.

They all waited patiently for what seemed like an hour. Finally a squad car pulled behind their truck. An officer, the one who Lacey's dad knew, walked up to the driver's side window. He said that they had caught the burglars trying to sneak out through the front. In fact, he had them in the back of his police car right there! The officer asked if Mr.Pinkerton and the girls would take a look at the burglars to see if they could identify them. Then he held up a black satchel.

"It looks like this is what they were after."

He reached into the bag and took out a slightly banged up golden barfing baby head sculpture. It had been smashed a bit so that the river of gold was now bent up into its face. The officer shook his head.

"I don't know why they would steal a valuable piece of art and then smash it like this. It

was ugly before, but now it's
ruined! Why would they do this?"

Lacey smiled proudly,

"I know exactly why. But first,
I want to get a look at these
perps!"

Lacey's dad led them over to the
back of the squad car so they
could get a good look. The
policeman shined his flashlight
into the car so they could see
better.

Lacey pointed at one of the men,

"It's Beardy! That's the guy
that was looking at the art when
we were here yesterday! But I
don't know who that other perp
is."

Her dad told the officer that he
recognized the bearded man as
well, but not the other "perp",
as Lacey had put it.

Sloan, still cradling the happy little dog, leaned in for a better look. Then she pointed at the second perp,

"Oh! I know *him*! That's the guy that works at the dog corral in the mall! He sometimes comes into my dad's store to buy dog treats. I'll bet that's how he got Mr.E inside!"

The policeman thanked them all for their extraordinary detective work. Mr.Pinkerton beamed with pride and put his arms around the two girls.

"It was all these two, I'm just the driver!"

Chapter 17

The Golden Beardy

Because it was late,
Mr.Pinkerton convinced the
police to wait until morning
before taking everyone's
statements. When Sloan got home
she had quite the story to tell,
but conveniently left out the
part where she jumped out of the
truck to save Mr.E. The police
never knew about the little
accomplice so Sloan took him
home. Her mom made him some
scrambled eggs and then gave him

a quick bath before sending him
and Sloan to bed. Both girls
were dreaming before their heads
ever hit the pillow.

Lacey had the strangest dreams!
She dreamed that she was at the
mall with Sloan. Newfus and Mr.E
were also there but they were
all dressed up in clothes from
Sloan's birthday party. The
really weird thing was that the
two dogs were *talking* to each
other! Newfus would suggest a
store where they had fabulous
bacon scented candles and then
Mr.E would comment on the
different potted plants he liked
to sleep behind. For some reason
they spoke with very proper
British accents.

When they reached the art
display everyone stopped to
admire the work. The paintings
in her dream were different from
the actual ones in the mall.

They were all various images of dogs posing like people. The strangest difference of all was the golden head sculpture. It wasn't a baby any more. It was the golden head of an old man! And the river of golden barf was now a shaggy golden beard. It was the old man who had told her that the display was so beautiful!

Mr.E, standing on his hind legs, was pointing and explaining to everyone about the hideous sculpture.

"You see, this lovey piece is called 'Golden Beardy' and is worth one million liver treats!"

Newfus, who was also standing on his hind legs, leaned down and adjusted his glasses to get a better look.

"I say old chum, that *is* an exquisite piece! May I lick it?"

Mr.E was more than happy to oblige,

"Indubitably! I'll join you!"

As the dogs took turns licking the distorted sculpture, Lacey and Sloan continued shopping. All the entrances to the stores had large security doors equipped with big green buttons to open them.

They saw a dress store that had a neon sign flashing in the window,

"Today Only, Everything FREE!"

As Lacey reached for the button she heard a voice behind her,

"I'll get that for you Lacey!"

It was Mr.E. He ran over and then stood up on his hind legs to push the button and let them into the store.

The dream continued on as the girls found several more "Everything FREE!" sales. Each time, Mr.E would push the button to let them in the stores! Suddenly there was a bright light and the dream faded away.

Lacey woke up and looked around. No huge bags of dresses and toys! She realized as she wiped the sleep from her eyes that it was all just a dream. The more alert and awake she became, the less she remembered from the dream. As she sat up in bed she couldn't remember anything from the crazy shopping spree.

Lacey's dad was adjusting his tie when she walked over to him. He looked down at his little detective.

"Well good morning sleepy head! You better jump in the shower and get ready. You have a big day today! The Chief of police *and* the Mayor are going to sit in when you give your statement! They want to meet you!"

Lacey perked right up.

"The Chief? *And* the Mayor? Really?"

Lacey ran wildly for the shower leaving a trail of socks and pajamas in her wake. She washed up and took extra time to brush her hair. She wanted to look her best so she asked her mom to help put in the barrettes. Lacey picked out a dress that she thought looked very businesslike and soon was ready to go.

Her dad was waiting at the bottom of the stairs with his keys and briefcase in hand.

"Are you ready sweetie? It's time to go."

Her father looked at her and was smiling from ear to ear.

"Oh Lacey, you look beautiful. So grown up!"

Her mother was standing by the kitchen, smiling proudly at her daughter. Mrs.Pinkerton looked as if she was going to cry. Lacey figured she must have been cutting onions in the kitchen.

"Yes daddy, I'm ready to go. Is Sloan coming too? And Newfus? Ok, probably not Newfus but I want Sloan to be there."

"No sweetie, Sloan is going with her dad to the pet store today and getting Mr.E all fixed up with shots and a microchip. Plus, *you* are the one who figured everything out and led the police to the thieves. As for Newfus, they actually *do* want us to bring him. Something about a commendation for saving that police officer last month. But the rest of the meeting today is all about you! They want to meet the junior detective who prevented a quarter of a million dollar art heist!"

Lacey knew that Sloan was exactly where she wanted to be. And Newfus was getting a commendation? The *Mayor* and the *Chief* both wanted to meet *her*! This was like a dream come true! Except that the dogs couldn't talk and everything at the mall wasn't free. Did she dream that? Lacey's mind was everywhere!

"Lacey? Hellooooooo? Are you coming?"

Lacey snapped out of her daze and followed her dad out the door. They loaded Newfus into the back of the truck being careful not to get fur all over their nice clothes. Lacey adjusted her seatbelt and they headed downtown.

When they reached the police station, Lacey took a deep breath to try and calm her nerves. Her dad put his hand on hers and told her,

"You'll be fine Lacey, don't be nervous. We'll take a secret way into the station so we don't have to walk Newfus in through the front. I'll have my office send some coffee and pastries to the conference room. Do you want anything?"

Lacey's stomach was in knots but she did think a bear claw sounded good.

"Chocolate milk and a bear claw for me… and a bacon maple bar for Newfus if that's ok?"

Her dad laughed,

"Of course it is. Now, let's go inside."

Her dad led them around the back of the station and swiped his security badge to get through a couple gates. The three of them entered the building through a door in the side of the building and walked down a hall. They arrived at a door marked "Conference Room" and Lacey's dad reached for the handle to open it. He looked over and saw Lacey straightening her dress and looking nervous. He waited to open the door and put his hands on her shoulders steadying her a bit.

"Lacey, remember we're the good guys. Good guys don't get nervous because they have nothing to hide. Be honest, speak from your heart and most of all, be yourself. I'm so proud of you!"

Lacey listened to every word but all she could really heard was her father saying "I'm so proud of you!". That was all she needed. Lacey reached out and opened the door herself.

Chapter 18

For Acts Of Bravery And Courage

She followed her dad into the
room looking for a place to sit
down. She had to pull a little
on Newfus's leash. He was
nervous around all the people in
such a small space. There were
several uniformed police
officers including the red
haired female officer that had
arrested Captain McNasty! She
smiled and waved at Lacey from
across the room. She saw her
dad's friend, who had arrested

the mall thieves. His name, she
found out later was Officer
Riggins. Lacey was already
feeling better. Officer Riggins
addressed Lacey in a very police
like voice. It was so serious
she thought.

"Miss Pinkerton, we have a seat
right here for you. Your dad can
sit next to you and we made a
bed over here by the wall for
Newfus. Do you think he will lie
down for a little while."

Lacey answered him,

"Oh, yes sir. He'll lay down
wherever I tell him to."

She led Newfus to the area where
a blanket had been laid out and
told him to lie down. The big
dog flopped down and bounced off
the base of the wall with a huge
thud, shaking the room.
Everybody laughed and Lacey
became a little embarrassed.

"I'm sorry, he's kind of clumsy. Maybe I should take him outside?"

A man with a big bushy mustache, dressed in a fancy looking police uniform stepped towards her.

"Nonsense! Newfus is a welcome guest of this police force. Lacey, I'm Chief MacArthur. It's a pleasure having you *and* Newfus here at my station. This big man standing behind me is Mayor Thompson."

The Mayor stepped toward Lacey with his hand stretched out, presumably wanting Lacey to shake it. Newfus jumped up and stood in between them, and barked. Every single person in the room including the Mayor jumped! Once again poor Lacey felt embarrassed.

"I'm really sorry Mr. Mayor, he's just a little over protective with all these people around. It's very nice to meet you! You should probably pull your hand back now. I don't want you to lose it because of me!"

The Mayor quickly withdrew his hand and laughed. Then the whole room laughed. This time Lacey laughed with them. The red haired female officer walked over and Newfus let her scratch his head. He must remember her thought Lacey.

"Hi Lacey, I never got to properly thank Newfus back at the crime scene last month. My name is Officer Ellen Stone, but you can call me Ellen. I brought something for the big guy that might help him relax."

She had a large grocery bag and pulled out an extra-large

rawhide bone. It was the size of Lacey's arm! The big dog started wagging his tail wildly sending papers flying and even whipping a few legs. Lacey made the giant dog sit down and be still as Officer Stone handed him his prize. She spoke directly to him. Lacey liked that a lot!

"I know it's just a dog treat but I wanted to thank you Newfus. If you hadn't disarmed that criminal, I might not have gone home to my own daughter and family. I also have this…"

She pulled a ribbon with a medal on it and placed it around his big neck.

"…for acts of bravery and courage in the face of danger. Thank you!"

Officer Stone gave Lacey a wink and a handshake before stepping back into the group of people waiting to hear Lacey's statement.

Now that Newfus was happily distracted by his new treat, Lacey went up to the Mayor and extended her hand. After a cautious look over at the big dog, he took her hand and shook it.

"Young Lady, you are one extraordinary individual. I have never in all my years seen someone so young solve a criminal case! And the Chief here tells me that you solved *two* in the last two months! Please have a seat and make yourself comfortable while we all get ready to hear your statement."

Chapter 19

Making A Statement

Lacey's head was buzzing from excitement. She was so nervous that she couldn't speak. All of a sudden her mouth was dry and she was hungry.

A young man came into the room with a large platter of pastries and a coffee pot with cups. He then brought Lacey a small container of chocolate milk and a bear claw on a paper plate. He also set a bacon maple bar down on a plate next to the bear claw. Lacey's dad gave her a wink and a smile. Lacey took a sip of milk and a big bite of the bear claw. She was starting to feel much better. Everyone served themselves and within a few minutes they were all seated around the huge conference table.

Lacey looked at all the faces looking back at her. She wasn't scared or nervous any more. The Mayor himself called her "extraordinary!" even *after* Newfus almost bit him! She looked at the microphone that was set up just in front of her and tapped it several times,

"Testing, testing….one two three…Is this thing on?"

"Not yet Lacey, I won't turn it on until you're ready."

It was Officer Riggins, Lacey was glad it was him taking the statement.

"It's nice to see you again Lacey. Here's how this will work, *you'll* be in charge. I'll ask you a few questions and you just do your best to answer them. After that, you'll give a statement and tell us the whole story from your point of view. If you want to take a break, we take a break. If you want another bear claw, then I will personally go get you one. Sound good?"

Lacey had just taken a large bite and wasn't expecting a question so soon. She just nodded and smiled.

Officer Riggins smiled back at her and continued,

"Ok Lacey I'm going to turn on the recording device now and everything we say will be on the official record, ok?"

Lacey was ready this time,

"Yes sir, I'm ready."

Officer Riggins flipped the switch on the recorder and began asking Lacey questions like her name, where she lived and other personal information. Then he asked her to tell the story from beginning to end on how the thieves had broken into the mall and how she figured out when they would be there?

Lacey began her statement with the events at the party and told everyone how they found Mr.E. She told them that she noticed how well trained the little dog was and how he was obviously trained to hide out of sight when in public, especially at the mall. Then she told them how she figured out what the black van connection was. She explained that she had looked up methods for melting gold and saw that it would be very easy for someone with the right equipment to melt down a large golden object. The same kind of equipment that had been stolen a

month earlier by the men in the
black van! When someone had
opened the automatic door for
her and Sloan, she hadn't given
it much thought. But then Mr.E
disappeared and she realized
that the men in the black van
had taken him. She figured that
Mr.E must have opened the door
both times. *Once* to let the
girls in and *again* to let the
thieves grab him. The poor
little guy was only doing what
they trained him to do. When
Lacey's dad had told her the
exhibit was being moved the next
day, she knew the thieves were
forced to break in that night.
They smashed the sculpture
because they had no intention of
trying to sell something so rare
and recognizable. The plan all
along was to melt it down and
sell the gold and jewels.

Chapter 20

A Great Reward

"So the hideous Golden Barf Baby sculpture was only as valuable as the stuff it was made out of."

A thin man with dark skin and large glasses raised his hand and smiled at Lacey.

"Well Miss Pinkerton, that isn't exactly accurate. Officer Riggins, may I speak for a moment?"

The man had a strange accent but Lacey couldn't quite place where it was from.

Officer Riggins told him that he could say a few things.

"Miss Pinkerton my name is Dr.Ramana Maharshi. I am the Indian Minister of Art and Culture as well as the curator of the National Art Museum in India. The 'Golden Barf Baby' as you call it has been an Indian national treasure for over one hundred years. It represents things that may seem silly to your culture, but it is absolutely irreplaceable. Its actual Indian name is the 'Ramsok'"

Lacey suddenly wished she had left out the word "hideous". The man must be very upset with her for insulting his culture like that.

The man smiled again and spoke with a voice that was very calm and kind.

"Please do not worry, I take no offense. This may be very undignified for an Indian to admit but when I first heard that you called the Ramsok a 'Golden Barf Baby' I laughed so hard that tea came out of my nose. The sculpture represents that which is unexpected and unpredictable yet joyous. It was only fitting that you should be the one that saved it from being lost forever."

Dr. Maharshi handed Lacey an envelope.

"What I have handed you is a check for fifty thousand dollars. It will be payable to your father but intended for you. Use it for tuition, a car, books or anything you wish. My country owes you a great debt of gratitude."

Lacey's dad started to protest but the man insisted.

"Please Mr.Pinkerton, the money is just a token of our appreciation. The reward we would have offered for the return of the artifact should it have been stolen, would have been twice as much. Miss Pinkerton, I hope our paths should cross again someday. I see great things in your future. I must now hurry to catch my flight home. I am bringing the Ramsok back to the museum. Artists and sculptors are standing by to have it repaired and back on display as soon as possible. I fear it will be a long time before America sees the Golden Barf Baby again. Thank you, and good day to you all."

Dr.Maharshi walked briskly from the room and was followed out by two assistants and a police escort.

Lacey was overwhelmed. First the Chief, then the Mayor, then Newfus got a commendation and now an Indian dignitary just gave her fifty thousand dollars? She pinched herself to see if she was dreaming. Nope, it hurt and she was awake.

Then she pinched her dad.

"OW! Lacey, what the heck?"

"Sorry daddy, I had to make sure I wasn't dreaming. Then I had to make sure I wasn't in one of your dreams either. This is just so much to take in!"

Lacey finished up her statement and then was asked to answer questions about Mr.E and what would Lacey do next.

"First, Mr.E was an innocent victim in all this. He was unlicensed, undocumented and legally available for adoption. My best friend Sloan Stevens, that's S-T-E-V-E-N-S, has adopted Mr.E through Second Chance Pets. He'll be loved, licensed, micro chipped and given a wonderful home."

Lacey paused and thought for a minute,

"As for me, I need to start preparing. In just one week, Sloan and I head out for Summer Camp! It's the first camp in the state that lets you bring your dog *and* lets them share in all the activities! I am going to use a little bit of the money from Dr.Maharshi to treat all my friends *and* their dogs to a week of fun, games and adventure! Most of all, NO mysteries!"

She turned to check on her own furry friend.

"Are you ready boy?"

Everyone looked down at Newfus who had eaten his *entire* giant rawhide. The enormous dog was laying on his back, sound asleep and snoring loudly. His medal was showing clearly on his chest so you could read the one word inscription.

It read: "HERO"

Lacey smiled proudly.

"Good Boy Newfus!"

The End (Of *this* adventure!)

20190311R00119

Made in the USA
Charleston, SC
29 June 2013